THAT
SILENT
SUMMER

THAT
SILENT
SUMMER

ELAINE MEDLINE

Artworks by Quin Brooks

GRANITE WINGS INC.

GRANITE WINGS INC.

GRANITE WINGS INC. EDITION, 2021
GraniteWings.com

First edition was published by Scholastic Canada Inc. in 1999.
Second Edition published by Granite Wings Inc. in 2021

Library and Archives Canada Cataloguing in Publication
Medline, Elaine, author
That Silent Summer / Elaine Medline

Softcover ISBN 978-1-7775922-0-2
eBook ISBN 978-1-7775922-1-9

e refer to it now. It's not the summer of
year. It's not the summer of the fire, or
ons disappeared, or the summer the fool
It's not any of those, although it could
remember every detail about The Sum-
e Paddle. It was awhile ago and I wasn't
he time. I'll try to include the important
ve anything out, you won't know about it
n't there. Already, I'm wondering whether
that time I kissed Nico Marchi. I don't
n though it was an important event. Use
. Not everything needs to be handed to
with parsley on the side.
r of the Purple Paddle was both a sad and
but it was more lovely than sad. In the
ve lived, I have never witnessed a summer
.
rt out so beautiful, though.
go home now," Minnow told us when she
or the first time. Her hair covered her eyes
nouth. It covered her entire face except for
was dripping tears that landed on the dirt
hutes from an airplane.
know what to say.
nterested in staying here," she said, her
ing.
't help but feel insulted, yet we knew the girl

Dedicated to my parents:
For their guidance, support and inspiration
through all the years

That's how w
such-and-such a
the summer the
built the castle.
have been. I don
mer of the Purp
taking notes at
facts, and if I lea
because you wer
to tell you abou
think I will, eve
your imaginatic
you on a platter

The Summe
lovely summer,
ninety years I h
so full of beaut

It didn't sta
"I'd like to
saw our cabin
and nose and
her chin, whic
like little para

We didn't
"I'm not
shoulders sha
We could

7

Minnow wore her
never combed, and
the sort of hair tha
Minnow vowed sh
the way it hid her
saying Minnow, but
We started calling l
good and natural sv
one at Birch Lake k
ple weren't even awa
name that wasn't hal

She arrived at ou
Purple Paddle.

had a point. What child would want to spend the summer with three relatives who were so old they were nearly dead? Minnow had met us only four times before, always at her home in the city. I suppose she thought we were strange, because she didn't talk to us much when we asked her questions, and she didn't hug us hello or goodbye. She was a city girl who lived in a high-rise and had never seen a loon. She was the kind of girl who liked highways and good restaurants and a house that was decorated in colors that matched.

If only she had looked around a bit more, that first day at the cabin. The hummingbirds were painting the air with their wings, but she didn't notice them. She didn't remark on the pink rocks lining the shore. She didn't hear the tree frogs screeching. She didn't feel the softness of the sun's heat on her feet and she didn't smell the hint of wild mint in the air.

"I won't stay more than a half-hour," she said. A toad squatted beside her toes but she didn't notice it. We beckoned her toward the cabin because we wanted to give her a tour, but she didn't move. That's when Yanny remembered the raspberry pie.

Yanny is Minnow's grandmother.

Yanny is also my little sister, born five years after me. You can remember Yanny because she's the one who bakes tasty pies and who loves canoes and rowboats and who wears fancy skirts.

Then there's Cliff.

Cliff is our younger brother, born five years after Yanny and ten years after me. He's the one lying in the hammock all the time. Sometimes Yanny and I call him Clifferbub. I don't know why. It's a nickname we gave him when he was just a baby.

Me, I'm Anna.

The three of us—Yanny, Cliff and I—lived together in our log cabin on top of a hill at the north end of Birch Lake. I was born there. I grew up there. I never left there.

Minnow asked if the raspberry pie was the type with crumble on top. When she learned it was, she finally budged from her spot and followed us into the cabin. We sat her down on one of the wobbly chairs around our kitchen table, then we presented her with a piece of pie and a glass of grape juice before she could take a look at the place and take off down the road. I really hoped she would like her piece of pie, just so I wouldn't have to listen to her say that she wanted to go home again.

"Thank you," she said politely as she placed her fork down neatly beside her plate. "But I'm not staying."

We pretended not to hear that. In truth, it was hard to take Minnow seriously at that moment, because her two top front teeth and the area to the right of her mouth were stained raspberry red.

We began the tour, starting with the living room. There were two couches in the living room, a brown cor-

CHAPTER TWO
Rowboat Ballet

"Today's a perfect swimming day," Yanny told Minnow. "The water in Birch Lake feels like silk. It's the most beautifulest water in the world."

When Yanny thought something was more beautiful than beautiful, she called it the most beautifulest. It wasn't good grammar, but she didn't care. Yanny tended to do things her own way.

On that day, the day after Minnow arrived at the cabin, Yanny was determined to get her granddaughter to enjoy Birch Lake. She grabbed Minnow's hand and hauled her down to the shore, warning her not to trip on the tree roots that spread across the path.

Thinking about that day still makes me chuckle.

You should have seen what Yanny was wearing. She was decked out all fancy, like she was trying to impress Minnow. She wore a pink cotton jacket and a pink short skirt, pink heels, pink pearl earrings the size of cherries and a pink pearl necklace to match. She looked like a wad of bubble gum or a bottle of nail polish or an overripe watermelon. Minnow examined Yanny from head to toe, then smirked at what she saw. Me, I wear sweats. Sweats are proper for a cabin. Skirts are not.

With Minnow following reluctantly, Yanny trundled down the dirt path to the shore, taking baby steps because of her heels. Yanny had sore knees, arthritis actually, which made it even harder for her to hoist herself over the tree roots.

We reached the shore without mishap, thankfully. Yanny walked to the end of the dock and held out her arms in front of her, palms to the sky. "Behold," she said, all dramatic. "The lake of lakes."

"I'm not swimming," Minnow said. She picked up a pink pebble and tossed it into the bushes behind her, acting like she couldn't care less about the lake of lakes. She didn't even stick a baby toe in the water.

"Look," Yanny said. "The loons. They're hiding in the reeds."

Sure enough, the two loons of Birch Lake were floating among the spiky green water plants called reeds. The loons had black backs covered in white polka dots. Their beaks were long and slender. Their eyes were red, red like bricks on an old farmhouse. You had to get pretty close in a boat to see their eyes. The same pair of loons returned to Birch Lake every summer. They paid us a visit on a daily basis. For us, watching them had become a hobby.

One loon disappeared under the water to forage for food. About half a minute elapsed and still that loon hadn't popped back up. Minnow stopped tossing pebbles and scanned the lake for the missing loon. She bit her nails, waiting for the loon to reappear.

Minnow suddenly let out a gasp of surprise. The loon had surfaced much farther out in the lake. Loons can swim underwater a long way without coming up for a breath, but I guess Minnow didn't know that. She's from the city, after all.

The other loon took a dive. Minnow pulled the hair out of her eyes so she could see better.

Yanny winked at me, as if to say, Things are going better with Minnow. It was obvious that Minnow liked the loons. And if she liked the loons, then she might like the lake. And if she liked the lake, she might have a good summer with us, even though she would have to go to the washroom in an outhouse without a window.

We heard a noise, a buzzing noise from across the lake. "Shhh," Yanny whispered.

The noise continued. It was, unmistakably, the sound of chainsaws.

Pay attention, because this noise isn't some insignificant detail I'm adding just to fill space. It's an important fact. I shudder as I write this part. That's because the source of this noise brought about terrible changes on the lake. Changes so terrible I don't even want to tell you about them, not yet anyway.

"I heard it yesterday, and the day before," Yanny fumed, her hands curled into fists. "Chainsaws. I think it's coming from Nico Marchi's place over in the next bay. I bet that man is cutting down trees. He's always complaining about his trees, about how they've become so big he's lost his view of the lake. Mark my words, he wants to destroy those trees. And they must be a thousand years old. Oh, it would be just like him."

I knew Nico Marchi, and I knew he wouldn't cut down his old pines and birches, even if they did block his view of the lake. There had to be another explanation. Truth was, I thought the world of Nico Marchi. He was a wonderful man. The best. He stayed fit too, often taking walks in the woods with his cane.

Yanny clutched Minnow by the wrist. "We're going to investigate," she said firmly.

"What?" asked Minnow, her voice shaky.

"We're going to get in the rowboat and row like ducks to Picnic Island, where we can see what's going on at Nico Marchi's place. And we're going to do it right now. I can't wait any longer. Nico Marchi must be stopped!"

"Can't we see Nico Marchi's place from here?" Minnow asked hopefully.

The answer was no. The Marchi place was around the corner, in the next bay, so it could only be seen from the middle of the lake, where Picnic Island was.

By now, Cliff had heard Yanny ranting. He got out of his hammock and joined us on the beach. His pants were crumpled and his hair stood straight in the air. He always looked like he had just woken up. When he heard what Yanny was about to do, he was flabbergasted, just as I was.

"Oh, for goodness sake, Yanny, let the girl relax," Cliff said. "She just arrived. Why don't you simply walk over to Nico Marchi's place and ask him about the chainsaws? Maybe he's not cutting down trees. Maybe he's just putting an extra room on his cottage."

"Go over to Nico Marchi's place?" Yanny laughed bitterly. "Cliff, that's impossible and you know it. I haven't talked to Nico Marchi in weeks. Ever since he made fun of my potted violets. I don't need to hear how my violets are droopy and his are more robust. I just don't need to hear that!"

Cliff sighed. "Perhaps it's coming from the old Edwards mansion," he said. "Maybe they're fixing up the old place."

"Oh, Cliff, that mansion has been deserted for ages. It's a wreck. Why would anyone want to have anything to do with it? Come on, Gabby, let's go for an adventure!" Yanny said, still holding her granddaughter's wrist. At that point, we still called Minnow Gabby. She hadn't earned her nickname yet.

Yanny kicked off her pink high heels. Grunting, she dragged the rowboat from the beach into the water.

"You row, Gabby. I'll be the passenger."

Minnow's mouth hung open.

"Just think of this little outing as a spy mission," Yanny whispered.

I touched Yanny's shoulder and pointed to the sky. Quite frankly, it looked like a storm was coming fast. The clouds were dark and heavy and ready to unload buckets of rain. The wind blew the leaves of the birches inside out. The waves looked like they were spitting saliva; it wasn't often there were so many whitecaps on Birch Lake. Yanny shrugged her shoulders. She didn't care about the weather. She was only interested in rowing to Picnic Island.

"Anna," she said to me, "you're overreacting. It's just a little cloud, minding its own business."

Fool that I was, I didn't stop her.

Instead, I decided to get in the rowboat with her and Minnow just in case they ran into trouble and needed help. Minnow put on her life jacket and took the oars. It was a wonder she went along with the plan, but I guess she couldn't resist the promise of a little action.

She was a bit like Yanny, as it turned out.

Minnow rowed just fine until she passed the protection of the reeds, which thrashed to and fro like a bunch of green fairies angry with the world. Beyond the reeds, the water became rough and Minnow made no progress.

The waves cancelled out her every pull on the oars. Water splashed in the boat. Yanny held her head high while the rain whipped her white hair.

"Not too much farther," she yelled, "that's the island there. It's a special island, Gabby. You'll love it. Your mother used to swim to it from our place. All that way. She was a great swimmer, your mother."

Minnow stopped rowing. She turned her head and stared at the island. "My mother swam all that way?" she asked.

"Every summer," Yanny said. Her face pulled into a frown. "Didn't she tell you?"

"No, never."

"Never?" Yanny asked, closing her eyes and taking a big breath, as if she was trying to calm herself.

"Never," Minnow repeated quietly. "Nothing."

"Well," said Yanny, "she swam to the island every summer. Her front crawl was flawless, so was her breaststroke, and she did the butterfly well, which not many can master. Your mother was a good swimmer. And every summer, she did the swim and we'd be there on Picnic Island to greet her, and we'd cheer, and the loons would cry out in celebration, and I'd do a little dance on the rock, which always embarrassed your mother to no end. Your Auntie Anna remembers those days, eh, Anna? Anna always rowed alongside your mother as she swam."

"Is that true?" Minnow asked me.

I nodded. I was the one who rowed beside Minnow's

mother during her yearly swim to Picnic Island. It was a grand privilege.

In the spring, a couple of months before Minnow arrived at the lake, Minnow's mother had sent Yanny a typed letter. The letter said: *Would you mind if Gabby spent the summer with you and Cliff and Anna? It would be good for her to get some fresh air in the country. I promise she won't be too much trouble.*

Did we mind? Of course not.

There was a P. S. at the end of the letter.

It said: *P. S. Maybe you could show her Picnic Island?*

Yanny could not believe her daughter had written such a letter. Minnow's mother, whose name was Marianne, was not a good letter writer after she left, not at all. Yanny wrote back right away, saying of course to send her, of course she wouldn't be any trouble.

Marianne never made an effort to visit us. Instead, we three very old people, with our bad backs and sore knees and all our other problems, had to drive in our station wagon for seven hours to visit her and Minnow. At least Marianne had the wisdom to send us Minnow for the summer.

Minnow's muscles were getting tired. She rowed more and more slowly until she gave up, dropping the oar blades on the gunwales, letting the boat drift upon the waves.

It was a bad case of rowboat ballet.

The loons edged up closer to us. One gave out a cry. It sounded like a snicker.

A large raindrop butted my forehead.

"We have to go back," Minnow told Yanny, "It's raining now."

"Let me row!" Yanny said.

"You can't," Minnow said, getting angry. "Let's turn back. I felt rain. We have to turn back. Please."

Yanny stuck out her tongue to test for rain. "It's not raining."

"It *is* raining," Minnow said.

"Let me row," Yanny repeated. "I'm strong. I have muscles. Look at my legs. These aren't the legs of an old lady. They're the legs of someone in her late sixties."

The waves were becoming more swollen. Yanny rose from her seat and was immediately thrown upon Minnow's lap. Minnow gently settled Yanny on the seat beside her.

"Okay, you row, but you won't get very far," Minnow said to Yanny, trying a new strategy to deal with her stubborn grandmother.

At this point, I had had enough. I tried to grab the oars from Yanny but she elbowed me in the ribs. Then I heard thunder.

"We better turn around now," Minnow begged. "Thunder."

"There's no stopping us now! That storm isn't anywhere near us."

Yanny, the fool, kept on rowing.

And then I heard another sound. At first I thought

it was more thunder, until I realized it was the sound of a motor. Cliff was coming to rescue us in the borrowed motorboat. I watched him as he steered the boat through a gap in the reeds and I thanked him under my breath. Before long, his boat sidled up to ours. He shook his head at Yanny in disapproval.

Yanny ignored him, crossing her arms across her chest and looking away. Cliff held out his hand to Minnow, helping her climb aboard the motorboat. He did the same for me. Yanny stayed in the rowboat, refusing to move. She never got into motorboats. She didn't believe in them. She said they scared the fish and birds. Why not just use a canoe or rowboat? she'd say.

Cliff tied a rope from the motorboat to the rowboat and towed Yanny back to shore. Yanny, true to form, sat proudly in the rowboat, looking like the queen of the lake being escorted back to her log castle. The waves hit the sides of our boats, sounding like applause.

As we docked, the storm began in earnest. Cold rain slammed down on our heads. Yanny's pink jacket and skirt stuck to her skin, making her look like a soaked pink rose. On the way up the hill, I stood behind her so that if she teetered backward she wouldn't roll down the path.

"Gabby," Yanny said to Minnow as we entered the cabin, "soon we'll try again, but next time we'll do it when Uncle Cliff is distracted. That way he won't rescue us for no reason. He only wants to act the hero! You and I are capable of rowing to Picnic Island by ourselves. We don't need Cliff to give us permission. He's younger than me! He has no right to take charge of my life. What does he want me to do? Sit inside the cabin and knit him a sweater every time there's a little drizzle?"

Then she added, slightly out of breath, "Anyway, we have to find out what Nico Marchi is up to. That's our goal, sweetie."

Minnow dragged herself to the brown corduroy couch, lay down, placed the back of one hand against her forehead, and sighed.

"I want," she murmured, "to go home."

CHAPTER THREE
The Pie System

Cliff lay on the hammock. He swung himself by kicking the trunk of a nearby birch tree.

"What's your favorite kind of pie?" he asked Minnow in the morning. Minnow didn't answer him. She still wanted to go home, I suppose, and she wasn't interested in making small talk.

"What's your favorite kind of pie?" Cliff asked again.

"Why?"

"Apple? Rhubarb? Sugar pie? Lemon meringue? Cherry? Boston cream? Petal of rose?"

"No such thing as petal of rose," answered Minnow, confused.

"Just checking to see if you were listening."

Cliff bent over to watch a line of ants scurrying over a dirt hill under the hammock. He leaned too far and fell out, landing on the ground with a thump. The ant hill, thank goodness, was spared in the mishap.

"Lemon meringue."

"Lemon meringue?" asked Cliff, dusting off his trousers. "Are you sure?"

"Yeah, why?"

"Why what?"

"Why are you asking me what type of pie I like?" asked Minnow, her voice filled with frustration.

"Oh, that. I'll tell you later. I'll let you in on a splendid secret."

Cliff closed his eyes. Before long, he was snoring. Minnow walked down the path toward the lake, wearing her swimsuit and carrying an old beach towel. I followed, as no one should be swimming alone.

She didn't swim right away, though. She went exploring on the shore, first to the left of our beach and then to the right.

To the left was our frog pond, where the little frogs sang their hearts out, sounding even better than the choir I once heard in the city when I dozed off for a bit because the music was so calming I forgot all my problems. Minnow stuck her feet in the pond. She heard a splash and ran away as fast as she could. It was only the sound of a frog jumping, but I guess it alarmed her.

When Minnow began exploring the area to the right of our beach, well, that's when she found the rock.

This wasn't just any old rock. This was The Rock, upon which many a person has thought about the meaning of life and the mysteries of the universe.

The Rock was gray and pinkish, the size of a small car. It had a flat top that was good for sitting on. You had to wade out to it and usually you'd get wet to your knees in order to get there. Up one side were small gouges that could be used for footholds.

Minnow climbed up to the top of The Rock, brushed some sand off with her towel, sat down cross-legged, bit her nails, and watched the loons ruffle their wings and take a few dives.

The Rock used to be a bit farther out in the lake. Every year, the winter ice moved it closer to shore. You should see Birch Lake in the winter. The birches and pines droop with curtains of ice. Wolf packs howl in the distance. And children play hockey, out on the frozen lake.

As I did, so many years ago.

In those days gone by—I have to explain this because I assume you're too young to have been around then—girls did not wear hockey skates. No girls wore hockey skates, except me. The skates I wore were hand-me-downs from my cousins. Since I had no female cousins—only a crowd of male cousins and a brother and sister much younger than me—I never owned a pair of figure skates.

CHAPTER FOUR
The Purple Paddle

Yanny hung up the phone. She left the cabin quietly without eating her piece of lemon pie.

Cliff followed to see what was the matter. He returned with his head bowed and told us that Maude Laska had passed away.

Yanny and Maude Laska had been best friends for almost seventy years, since they were twelve or thirteen. When they were young, Yanny and Maude canoed together and swam together and built sand sculptures in the shape of frogs and birds and sat on the dock for hours and hours, talking and laughing and staring at the sky.

Yanny would lecture Maude all the time on how to canoe better and how to swim better and how to build better sculptures. Maude would listen politely, then ignore the advice and carry on doing what she'd been doing the way she had been doing it all along. Oh, they were a pair, Maude and Yanny.

Maude died in her sleep in her tiny shack across the lake, near the town. She was old when she died, and she had been sick for more than a year, but it was still a shock to learn she was gone. Never again would Yanny, Cliff and I play cards with Maude Laska late into the night. Those gin rummy games, I'll never forget them. The game usually ended with Maude calmly declaring, "I shall not play with a person who cheats at cards." She meant Yanny. Yanny was a terrible cheater.

Yanny would then reply, "I refuse to play with someone who calls me a cheater," and the game would end unfinished and we'd have to find something else to do like play charades or work on a jigsaw puzzle. We never finished our jigsaw puzzles because a quarter of the pieces were always missing.

Too bad Minnow didn't have the chance to meet Maude Laska. Minnow would have liked her. Everyone did.

On the day of the funeral, Yanny refused to get out of bed. Poor Cliff had to lift her up and plop her on her chair and coax her into getting dressed. Yanny's face was wet with tears and the bags under her eyes sagged. Her shoulders were hunched. When she combed her hair, chunks of it came out on the brush.

I helped her get ready for the funeral, ironing her black skirt and black blouse and shining her shoes.

"All my friends are gone," she said.

"You've got lots of friends, Yanny," said Cliff, unfortunately adding, "what about Nico Marchi?"

That was the wrong thing to say. Nico Marchi, of course, was the man who had poked fun at Yanny's violets. Yanny and Nico used to be friends, until that Big Violet Fight, as we called it.

But maybe it was a good subject to bring up, after all, for Yanny stopped crying. She stared at Cliff, pursing her lips. "Nico Marchi," she uttered, "is not my friend."

By the way, here's some advice for you if you ever meet Yanny. Compliment her on her violets, even if they look lousy. And they do look lousy, believe me. Withered and dry and rarely blooming. Compared to my gladiolas, Yanny's violets were pathetic.

Minnow was supposed to stay alone at the cabin while we attended the funeral. We felt she was old enough and we were pretty sure she wouldn't take off on us. But she insisted on coming along.

"Absolutely not," Yanny said, shaking her head. "It's not the sort of thing a child should do on a sunny afternoon. You should stay here and build an elaborate sandcastle. Or sit on The Rock and watch the loons."

"But I want to go to the funeral," Minnow insisted.

At the time, we had no idea why she wanted to go

to the funeral. Funerals aren't events that kids usually beg to go to. But looking back, I think Minnow wanted to give some emotional support to Yanny, who was so sad. Minnow was a generous girl, as it turned out, often doing good deeds for people. Holding Yanny's hand at the funeral was one of those good deeds. When she first arrived at the cabin, we thought she was a miserable runt. Only later did we realize she showed her affection in her own quiet way.

I don't know what made Minnow start liking life at the log cabin. Maybe it was the loons, or the swimming, or The Rock, or the pie system. Or perhaps Yanny's sadness made Minnow see her own problems as less important.

"Why on earth do you want to come?" Yanny asked Minnow. "It might depress you."

But Minnow kept on insisting, so Yanny gave in.

"Okay, come along then, Minnow, but I'm not in favor of it," said Yanny. "You didn't even know my friend Maude, may she rest in peace. Maude loved to canoe, you know. I was much better at canoeing than her, of course. She never did get the hang of it, even though I tried to teach her a proper J-stroke. I always took the stern, and she took the bow, because she was the weaker paddler. We sometimes paddled out to Picnic Island for picnics. We ate her home-made bread with her homemade marmalade. She was a good cook. You and I should try to get to Picnic Island again, Minnow, when the sky is clear. There's still quite a bit of chainsaw noise coming from the next bay. It's odd. I don't understand why it's been going on for so long."

When we are all in the station wagon, Yanny apologized, saying she had to run back to the cabin because she had forgotten her extra pair of underwear.

Yanny was incontinent. That meant she didn't make it to the bathroom in time to pee sometimes. And Yanny, being Yanny, refused to wear adult diapers, so she carried an extra pair of underwear in her purse. Then if she had an accident, she simply made a quick change of underwear. Cliff explained all this to Minnow as we waited for Yanny in the car. Minnow looked disgusted, like she didn't want to hear about it. I don't blame her. It's hard on a kid to be around three old people all the time, learning about their problems. Yanny, Cliff and I were as old as rocks and we weren't getting any younger.

The cemetery was in a clearing surrounded by pine trees. About fifty mourners came. Pine needles carpeted the ground. The smell of those pine needles wafted through the air like perfume. If you had to be buried, this was a nice place to have it done. Yanny was crying the hardest of anyone. When her nose started running, she reached into her purse to fetch a handkerchief. She blew her nose into what she thought was a handkerchief. But it wasn't.

"Yanny," Minnow whispered loudly.

Yanny stared at Minnow, frowning. "Shhh, Minnow. Don't talk during the prayers."

"But—"

"Later."

Minnow's shoulders began to shake with laughter. I had to stop myself from laughing also. When the prayers ended, Nico Marchi—supported by his cane—approached Yanny and patted one of her shoulders.

Yanny moved away from him. By now she had stopped crying and was about to put her handkerchief—or what she thought was a handkerchief—back into her purse when a look of shock came over her face. She realized that the item she had been crying into wasn't a handkerchief at all.

She quickly shoved her underwear back into her purse. "Getting old is for the birds," she said to no one in particular.

After the service, Maude Laska's sister approached Yanny, saying, "Maude left this to you in her will. She made it herself, you know. From scratch."

Yanny was so touched that she began to cry again. Swaying her body, she hugged the gift tight to her chest.

"The purple paddle!" she cried. "I watched Maude make it. It meant so much to her."

That night, after supper, Yanny placed the purple paddle on the fireplace mantel.

We all sat on the brown corduroy and orange corduroy couches sipping hot chocolate and admiring the purple paddle. Everyone had a comment about it.

"I like the color," Minnow said. "It's better than plain wood."

"The paddle has personality," Cliff said. "More personality than any paddle that anyone has ever dipped into Birch Lake."

Yanny said, "I told Maude to fix the part of the blade that's crooked, but she didn't."

Minnow stared at me, right in the face.

"What do you think about the paddle, Anna?"

Yanny gulped.

Cliff raised his bushy eyebrows in surprise.

I felt like running from the room.

"It's bedtime, Minnow," Yanny said.

But Minnow didn't move.

"Why can't you talk, Anna?" she asked.

CHAPTER FIVE
Did You Ever Talk?

I said nothing.

"Minnow, it's bedtime," Yanny repeated.

Minnow looked at me with eyes that asked too many questions. "Anna, why don't you ever talk? Can you talk if you wanted to? Did you ever talk?"

I shrugged my shoulders and gave her a weak smile. She was a persistent girl. I'll give her credit for that.

Truth be told, I stopped talking years and years and years ago, and I really don't want to give you more details at the moment. They could be the subject of another story if I ever did write another one. But this story isn't about me, as you're aware by now, so let's get on with it.

The next day, the day after the funeral, things were

getting back to normal. Yanny was still sad, of course. She often looked at the purple paddle and sighed. Cliff lay in the hammock as usual. Minnow sat on a tree stump near the hammock, chewing on a piece of grass.

I admired my gladiolas. Gladiolas are the most glorious flowers that exist. They're made up of green stalks, taller than my waist, bursting with flowers from top to bottom. Every year I win the first-place ribbon at the fair for the nicest gladiolas. Or did I already tell you that? I can't always remember everything. Sometimes I worry I'll end up like my friend Sue Gomely. You don't know her. She lives in a nursing home in town. She doesn't recognize anyone anymore. She doesn't know what day of the week it is. It's like an eraser got hold of her mind.

So there I was, admiring my gladiolas, and I couldn't help but listen to the conversation going on between Cliff and Minnow.

"Don't you get bored, lying on a hammock all day?" Minnow asked Cliff.

"Bored? Not really. There's so much to do on this hammock."

"Like what?" Minnow asked.

"Like watching the sun move from east to west."

Minnow rolled her eyes and laughed.

"Like writing my 100-page poem," Cliff added.

"You're writing a 100-page poem?" Minnow asked, astonished.

"I am," he said. "And don't you dare ask me when I'm going to finish it. Everyone asks me that question. It's a question I refuse to answer."

Minnow paused, then asked, "when are you going to finish it?"

Cliff mussed her hair, which was quite mussed to begin with.

"What else?" she asked.

"What else what?"

"What else do you do to keep yourself from getting bored?"

"Fall asleep to the buzz of dragonflies. Feel the sun warm my face. Daydream."

"Daydream about what?"

"About blueberries overflowing from baskets sold from the backs of trucks on the highway."

"Why doesn't Aunt Anna talk?" Minnow asked.

My ears perked up like a bunny's. Cliff and Minnow didn't know I was listening, so I stood still and tried not to rustle the gladiola stalks.

"She doesn't talk?" Cliff joked. "I hadn't noticed."

"Be serious," Minnow said. "There has to be a reason why a person doesn't talk."

"Well," said Cliff, "you could try asking her again."

"That's kind of difficult, when she can't talk."

"I have a question for you, Minnow," Cliff said. "Do loons like us as much as we like them?"

"Loons hate us, probably," she said. "They probably hate our motorboats."

"Minnow, tell me this. What do you like better, pine trees or maple trees?"

She said maple trees because you can get maple syrup out of them. He said pine trees because they're green all year around.

"Minnow, if you could own only one thing, what would it be?"

She said Bow Bow Pom Pom.

I haven't told you about Bow Bow Pom Pom. Minnow slept with this clown she called Bow Bow Pom Pom and Bow Bow Pom Pom usually ended up on the floor by morning. I guess Bow Bow Pom Pom gave her comfort, just like the purple paddle offered Yanny some solace. Bow Bow Pom Pom had lost most of its black pom poms that were attached to its clown hat and clown shoes. The golden bow around its neck had also disappeared, so long ago that Minnow said she couldn't remember it. Bow Bow Pom Pom was a dirty ratty thing, which Minnow loved.

"No more questions," Minnow told Cliff. "I'm going for a swim. Who will watch me?"

"Anna will," said Cliff. "She's hiding behind her gladiolas."

He'd caught me. I stepped out from behind the flowers and trekked with Minnow down the path to the lake. Minnow ventured into the water gradually, gasping each time she took a step forward because the water was cold. She counted from three to one backwards and dove forward, ducking her head and starting the front crawl.

She was a good swimmer, just like her mother.

Minnow's mother Marianne loved swimming to the island, but she didn't like much else about Birch Lake. In fact, she left home when she was only a teenager, after her father Charlie died in an accident. That accident was a terrible thing; don't ask me about it because there's nothing good to tell.

Marianne was an only child, so that left Yanny and her all alone in town after Charlie's death. Staying in the house that Charlie built, without Charlie, was tough on Yanny. She repainted the wood shingles, changing the color from light blue to mauve. She switched bedrooms with Marianne. She bought a piano, took three lessons and quit. She tried to adjust, but it wasn't any good; she had to get out of there. And where was there to go except back to the cabin, the place where Yanny had grown up, the place where she had lived waiting for Charlie to return from the war? The place she loved best? When she announced to Marianne that they would sell the house in town and move in with me and Cliff, Marianne told her mother she should try painting the shingles again.

To make a long and painful story short, Marianne just refused to move to the cabin. True, she had spent summer weekends there, but that was about all she could take.

Full-time at the cabin isn't for me, Marianne said. I'm not going in an outhouse in the winter, she said. I won't share a room with my mother, she said. When we suggested she sleep on the couch, she laughed. Come to think of it, she never complimented me on my gladiolas, and she never joined in Cliff's discussions about the beauty of loons and the wonder of insects.

And Yanny, she never truly appreciated Yanny. Calm down, be quiet, have some dignity, she often told her mother. You're a laughingstock, she once said.

Yanny and Marianne were like oil and vinegar in a cup of salad dressing that hasn't been mixed yet. Just naturally separate, somehow. They were both stubborn, that was for sure. Yanny wouldn't back down and neither would her daughter.

The day before they were supposed to move to the cabin, Marianne packed a khaki canvas knapsack—one that had belonged to her father—and marched off in the direction of the bus station. Yanny chased her down the street.

I heard this sorrowful tale afterward, when a very vexed Yanny recounted it to me.

"Where do you think you're going?" Yanny demanded.

"The city," Marianne said simply.

Yanny ran to keep up with Marianne—and that wouldn't have been an easy thing to do in high heels, which of course Yanny always wore.

"You won't," Yanny said.

"Yes, I will," Marianne said firmly.

"I won't allow it."

"Doesn't matter."

That's how they talked to one another.

"You like the cabin," Yanny said, when they had arrived at the bus station. "I know you like the cabin. What about swimming to Picnic Island? You never complained about that! What about that?"

"What about it?" Marianne said, striding toward the bus.

"You like my pies!" Yanny yelled. "You can't tell me you don't like my pies!"

Marianne climbed up the bus stairs and turned to face her mother. "What do pies have to do with anything?" she said.

Actually, Marianne did like Yanny's pies, especially her lemon meringue pies, but she would never admit it.

"You'll come back!" shouted Yanny. "You'll come back, Marianne. I know you will. It's better here than there!"

The bus door skreeked shut.

"Come back, Marianne," Yanny whispered, and the bus disappeared down the dusty road. Where it took her, that's where Marianne stayed.

Minnow had reached the reeds. I clapped. She heard my clapping, waved to me, and smiled. She swam back to shore and climbed on top of The Rock, drying herself in the sun. Meantime, I lifted a few big rocks from the bottom of the lake and lugged them to shore. I planned to encircle the rocks around a new flower garden. Not for gladiolas, since I had enough gladiolas, but for yellow snapdragons or pink roses or white daisies.

I heard hammering and sawing in the next bay. Something was going on, no doubt about it, something that would alarm Yanny for sure.

Speaking of Yanny, she appeared on the shore just as I had finished lifting my last rock out of the lake. She was carrying three paddles—the purple paddle, a cracked wooden paddle and a kid's paddle. She wore a life jacket over a flowery dress flowing down to her ankles. That was Yanny all right, wearing fancy clothes for a jaunt in the canoe. The woman didn't even own a pair of pants.

"Let's go canoeing, Minnow," Yanny shouted. "You, too, Anna. We'll paddle to Picnic Island. We'll find out what all that noise is about." Not again, I thought.

"Not again," Minnow said, echoing my thoughts.

Yanny kept the purple paddle for herself and gave me the cracked paddle and Minnow the kid's paddle. Yanny took the stern because she liked to steer. I took the bow, and Minnow sat cross-legged in the middle. The reeds brushed our hands and faces as we paddled through them. The water was calm and the sky was clear. Thankfully, there would be no rain or thunder on this trip to the island.

"Anna," Yanny said. "You're lilydipping."

Lilydipping meant I wasn't paddling hard, which wasn't

true. I was making little whirlpools in the water every time I pulled my paddle, which meant I wasn't lilydipping.

"Minnow, sit more in the middle," said Yanny. "You're tipping the canoe a bit to the left."

Minnow shifted, tipping the canoe to the right now.

"Anna, you're still lilydipping."

I wished she'd leave me alone. I wasn't lilydipping. I wished I could talk. Then I could defend myself against Yanny's rants.

"Minnow, did I ever tell you about the time that Maude and I spent the night on Picnic Island? We were about fifteen years old at the time."

Good, a story. A story was better than Yanny's complaints.

"There were a lot of mosquitoes that night," Yanny said. "We slept under wool blankets on the moss next to our bonfire, under the stars. It was a strange, strange night. That's good, Anna, your stroke is improving."

My stroke wasn't any different than it was a minute before.

"There were so many mosquitoes we had to hide our heads underneath our blankets. Even so, they crept into our ears and bit us there. It had been a damp summer, so the mosquitoes were around later in the season than usual. What I'll never forget were the loons, though. There must've been about fifty loons gathered near the island that night. It was quite unusual to have so many loons in one place. I suppose they were getting ready to migrate south for the winter together. The loons were calling back and forth, back and forth. Loudly. We could barely carry on a conversation, their cries were so loud."

"Wow," Minnow said. "Fifty loons."

"Maude behaved oddly that night," continued Yanny. "You won't believe this when I tell you, but she got out from under her blanket and started running around the campfire, tears dripping down her face. Her hands covered her ears. She screamed the word 'loons' about a dozen times. The mosquitoes and the cry of the loons were making her frantic and frenzied, I suppose."

Minnow stopped paddling so she could laugh.

"I know it sounds funny when I tell it now. But at the time, I was terrified. I was worried about Maude's welfare. When she finally stood still, I put my arms around her, patted her head and told her that everything was all right. After awhile she got back under her blankets. By then she was exhausted and she fell asleep. And while she slept I remember thinking how strange it was to create such a fuss about a bunch of loons, a bunch of silly loons! Who cared about a bunch of loons?"

Yanny interrupted her story to tell Minnow to keep paddling and to tell me I wasn't holding my paddle properly.

"But the next day," she went on, "I thought about it more and I decided the loons weren't silly at all. The call of those loons was the most beautifulest thing I had ever heard. After hearing the cry of those loons, suddenly everything else seemed more beautiful—the rocking chair on the cabin porch, my father's work shirts drying on the clothesline, my mother's favorite bowl for mixing bread dough. My brother seemed nicer and he was horrible back then. Even my face seemed prettier, and I was never a good-looking girl, if I must be honest, although my legs were always something to admire. Oh, I'll never forget the call of those loons! It sounded like a symphony of flutes. But better than flutes. It was like hearing something from another planet. All the joy and all the suffering in the world could be heard in the call of those loons. It sounded like crying. It sounded like laughter. It sounded like crying and laughter at the same time."

We arrived at the island just as Yanny finished her story. I stepped out of the canoe into ankle-deep water, then dragged the boat onto a large flat rock that sloped from the shore into the lake. That's the job of the bow person—to get the canoe safely on shore.

Minnow and Yanny stepped onto dry land. From where we stood, we couldn't see the bay where the noise was coming from, so we walked to the other side of the island over an overgrown path, past the lone jack pine.

Finally, we would find out what was causing the noise. My curiosity grew with each step along the path. If Nico Marchi was chopping down his trees, which I doubted, Yanny would never forgive him.

But nothing could have prepared us for what we saw. We stood there, stunned.

"Ooh," Minnow said.

"Incredible," I thought.

Yanny shook her head. "Oh, no," she said, in a whisper. "Oh, no."

CHAPTER SIX
Oh No

Yanny placed her fingers over her lips, as if trying to stop herself from crying out in despair.

"Ooh," Minnow whispered again, biting her nails. The noise hadn't come from Nico Marchi's place after all. Nico hadn't cut down his trees. Nor had he added a room to his cottage. There was another reason for all the sawing and hammering we had heard lately, and it was something we had never predicted.

"Get back in the canoe," Yanny ordered us. "Paddle like geese. I want to take a closer look."

Yanny dragged the canoe back into the water, hiked up her dress, and sat herself down in the stern. Minnow and I got in. We paddled without saying a word.

Before we reached shore, Yanny said, "Stop," and we let the canoe drift while we looked upon a site that astounded us all.

In front of us, in place of the old Edwards mansion, stood a castle so high it seemed to shove the clouds upward and so wide it appeared to kick the woods off to the side. It was a white-gray color, the color of moths. It cast a shadow on the Marchi cottage, which was right next door in the same bay.

The castle's lawn was so finely mown it looked like it had been given a crew cut. About a dozen wooden chairs were stacked in three piles on the lawn. The chairs were too new, not weather-beaten as I prefer. A dock stretched out to the reeds, long enough to bowl on. Its fresh green paint glistened. Lining the beach were a bunch of motorboats and those little noisy boats that skim across the water like little brats. What they're called I don't remember. They're like Ski-Doos, but for water, not snow.

We heard voices, muffled so that we couldn't make out the words. They were coming from two men who were perched on ladders, hanging brightly colored lanterns around one of the turrets of the castle.

"It's so pretty," Minnow said.

"Minnow," Yanny said, her voice shaking, "what is this castle made of, do you think?"

"Some sort of white stone?" Minnow guessed.

"I'm not sure," Yanny said. "Let's go on shore."

Minnow hesitated. "Are we allowed?" she asked.

"I don't care if we are or we're not," Yanny said. "I've lived on this lake for more than eighty years, and nobody can tell me where I can walk. Why have we never heard about this? I never gave my permission for this monstrosity to be built!"

That was Yanny, all right, thinking she was queen of the lake. As if people needed *her* permission to build a castle.

Yanny stomped across the lawn to the castle. She peered at its white walls, touching them gently with the tips of her fingers. "Oh, no," she said. "Oh, no." Her eyes filled with tears.

"What's the matter?" Minnow asked her grandmother. "A castle on the lake's not so terrible. It's kind of nice. It sparkles."

Yanny walked away from the castle to the birch woods behind. She patted the trunks of the birches, muttering, still crying. She ran from tree to tree, as if in a daze. We still couldn't understand why she was upset.

We too looked at the birches, and then we saw what Yanny saw.

The bark of each and every birch tree was stripped off. The trees looked naked without their bark. They seemed to be in pain. They were shivering. Their leaves were already turning yellow around the edges, because, as everyone knows, a birch tree can't survive without its bark.

Yanny ran back to the castle. We followed. She grabbed

one of Minnow's hands with her own hands. She ordered her to feel the walls of the new building. She ordered me to do the same. The walls felt papery.

"Birchbark!" exclaimed Minnow.

This was a castle covered in birchbark. Someone had covered the old Edwards mansion with birchbark, adding a few turrets to make it look like a castle.

"They must have stripped every birch tree they could get their hands on to get this much bark," said Yanny. "How could they do this? Who did it? Why?"

We walked to the front of the birchbark castle. The front door, which was also covered with birchbark, had been left open. We tiptoed inside. The first thing we saw was a curved staircase coated in birchbark.

"I'd like to climb that staircase," Minnow whispered to me.

I must admit here and now, that at that point I found the castle charming, just as Minnow did. Of course, I was upset about the birch trees, that goes without saying. Yet the castle was stunning. It did sparkle. I saw its beauty, as did Minnow. Yanny refused to see it; she recognized only the ugliness that the castle had wreaked on the surrounding woods. As it turned out, the castle wasn't all that great, as you'll see. Don't be fooled by some fancy colorful lights wrapped around a fancy turret. Don't be fooled by a nice lawn and an extended dock and an irresistible front door. Don't be fooled like I was.

To the right of the entranceway was a large room where a few workers were unpacking crystal glasses from a box. The men didn't notice us. Several tables, with what looked like a veneer of birchbark, were piled in a corner. This was obviously the dining room. Attached to the ceiling, near the bar, was a television set. Minnow pointed it out to me, smiling behind Yanny's back.

"I've seen enough," said Yanny. "Let's go."

"Can't I climb the staircase?" Minnow pleaded.

"Absolutely not."

"Please?" Minnow asked, walking toward it.

"You go up that staircase," Yanny said, "and you are not my granddaughter."

Minnow stopped abruptly, aghast and dismayed. I was also shocked by what Yanny had said. Minnow turned around slowly to face me, rolled her eyes toward the ceiling, and giggled nervously at Yanny.

"Uh, okay," she said.

"We're going to speak with Nico Marchi," Yanny announced.

"Okay," Minnow repeated.

To reach the Marchi place we had to wade through a frog pond. The pond was warm and mucky, a comfort to our feet. Nico was sitting on the steps of his porch, reading the newspaper under the shadow of the castle.

"Nico, what's going on next door?" Yanny demanded.

"I thought you weren't talking to me," Nico said without looking up.

"Never mind that now. Why didn't you tell me what was going on here?"

He said nothing.

"Nico," Yanny said, "talk to me."

Nico finally looked at Yanny and said, "For weeks you haven't given me the time of day, so why should I talk to you now?"

He folded his newspaper, got up from his chair and hobbled into his cabin. We followed.

Nico opened a cupboard and reached for a can of baked beans. He opened the drawer under the oven and removed a pot.

"Who stripped the birches?" Yanny asked.

Nico stirred the beans with a spoon. For the first time, he took notice of Minnow.

"I haven't yet been introduced to this young woman," he said. "She must be the granddaughter you talk about so much."

Nico held out his hand to Minnow.

"I'm Nico Marchi," he said. "I saw you at the funeral."

"I'm Gabby," Minnow said shaking his hand. "But everyone here calls me Minnow."

"Pleasure to meet you, Minnow. Did you know that my great-granddaughter arrives in a couple of weeks? It will be her first time here. She lives so far away. The two of you can romp around together. She's about your age. Anna, so glad you could visit. You look wonderful."

I beamed. Nico Marchi, at eighty-five years old, was handsome and strong. His wife had died years and years ago and he never remarried. All the elderly women on the lake ogled him. Not a hair on his head, but his baldness made him look all the more savvy. Unlike the other women on the lake, I knew I had no chance with him. Who would want to date a person who couldn't talk? But my love life is no business of yours, and I don't know why I'm sharing it with you.

"Nico," Yanny said, irritated, "we have been friends our whole lives and you didn't have the decency to tell me about this ecological disaster next door to you?"

"You must be the last to know. Really, you are out of touch, Yanny. That castle has been the talk of the town. Where have you been? You haven't come by my cabin in a dog's age, and I don't even know why you're mad at me."

"You do know, Nico Marchi."

"Really, I don't."

Nico sauntered over to his violets. He touched their leaves, felt their soil and gazed at them lovingly. As you might remember, the violets were the cause of the fight between Yanny and Nico. And here he was fawning over his violets, bringing attention to their beauty. Oh, Nico knew how to irritate Yanny. But Yanny didn't really care about the violets anymore. She had something more pressing to worry about—the castle.

"Okay, listen," Yanny told Nico. "Let's put our little disagreement behind us. I agree, your violets are nicer. That's that then. Your violets are nice, and mine aren't. Are you happy now? Look, we've got to do something about that abomination they've constructed on our lake, do you hear? Let's think. We've got to stop it. They've already killed all the birches!"

"Yanny, you're being so unrealistic. There's nothing we can do. The castle is built. We don't own the land. Things change. Did you really expect the lake to stay the same forever?"

Yanny's bottom lip was shaking.

"Yanny," said Nico. "You've got to calm down. I'll tell you everything I know. But first, calm down. Maybe a glass of sherry will help. I've got a bottle hidden away. Anna, will you pour three glasses, please?"

He winked at me. Nico Marchi winked at me.

Yanny settled into an armchair while Nico told her what he knew about the castle.

"The castle is going to be a conference center, a meeting place for businesspeople. The guests will attend meetings but they'll also relax and go swimming and boating and water-skiing, etcetera. The castle opens officially in a couple of weeks. They're still working on getting the inside ready. So our sleepy little lake will be shaken up a bit."

Yanny nodded, sipping the sherry.

"When the birch trees were stripped for the bark, a lot of folks around the lake were pretty upset. But no one protested, at least not to the castle's owner. People are hoping they'll get a job at the castle, you see. And you've got to admit the castle is beautiful. To be truthful, it enhances the lake, in my opinion. It gives it a mystical feel, don't you think? The owner—I've never met her. I don't even know if she's here yet. So, there you go. That's all I know."

Yanny moaned.

"Yanny, you can't let it get to you, really." He pointed at his newspaper. "Newspapers are made of trees as well. Condemning the castle would be hypocritical of me. Would you like some beans, any of you?"

The canoe ride had made us hungry, so we ate heartily before paddling home.

That night, Yanny went to bed early, saying she was too upset to stay up and pretend all was well, when all wasn't well.

After Yanny had gone upstairs, Minnow had a suggestion. It was a good suggestion. Minnow proposed we make a pie for Yanny. Minnow was a good kid. She really was. She didn't say a whole lot, but she did good deeds for people and I respected that.

We made Yanny a rhubarb pie, her favorite. I found a recipe in one of Yanny's cookbooks, its pages stained with ingredients from meals made over the decades. Minnow's job was to cut the rhubarb—almost our last rhubarb of the season—and measure out the flour. I noticed Minnow swishing her hands inside the flour bin for a minute or two. Ah, the feel of flour! Such a comfort. Cliff measured out the rest of the ingredients. I made the pastry and supervised the entire operation.

It wasn't a great-looking pie. For starters, we burned the crust. It certainly didn't look like the sort of pie Yanny would make. Still, it was a pie. And any pie is better than no pie.

Minnow led the way upstairs to Yanny's bedroom. Yanny was already asleep, lying on top of her covers in her clothes.

Quietly, we placed the pie on her dresser. She didn't wake up.

We tiptoed downstairs. Cliff and I tucked Minnow into bed. We kissed her good night, as well as Bow Bow Pom Pom, for goodness sake.

"Good night, Minnow," we sang, "good night, Minnow. Good night, Minnow, it's time to say good night."

Then we pulled up a pair of wobbly kitchen chairs around the card table and had ourselves a couple of games of gin rummy. Cliff won a game and I won a game, and we were too tired to play another one to break the tie.

CHAPTER SEVEN
Bitten Nails

The days passed. Every day, Minnow swam a bit farther. Her muscles became stronger, her kick more forceful. I showed her how to turn her head more efficiently to take a breath, and her rhythm was improving.

I'll never forget the day Minnow asked me the big favor. That was also the day that she mentioned my tattoo.

Minnow began the day with a swim. She always started her swim with the front crawl, then switched to breast-stroke, then side stroke, then elementary backstroke. In elementary backstroke, you swim like a frog on its back. It's a restful stroke, but it's hard to get your legs coordinated just right. Me, I like the side stroke because it's the easiest in my opinion, and you don't swallow as much water.

Minnow reached the reeds, then rested there by treading water. I clapped, as I always did when she reached the reeds. She waved, giving me a thumbs-up.

I had become Minnow's designated lifeguard, her unofficial swimming coach.

The two loons of Birch Lake were also her coaches, in a way. They watched her calmly with their red eyes, taking the occasional dive into the muck at the bottom of the lake to search for crayfish, sometimes standing up in the water and flapping their wings, sometimes calling out with their strange cry. The loons had become Minnow's companions in the water, just like Bow Bow Pom Pom was her companion at night. The way she clung to that tattered clown! A sock stuffed with stuffing, wearing a green and orange clown suit and no bows or poms to speak of. But I must be honest. I was starting to like Bow Bow Pom Pom. So floppy and modest, not show-offy like some plastic skinny rinky doll with a sequin dress. The clown needed a good washing, though.

Minnow swam back to shore slowly. I waited for her with a towel.

"Aunt Anna," she said as she dried herself, "before the summer is over, I'm going to swim to Picnic Island."

I couldn't have been more pleased. Minnow was going to swim to Picnic Island, just like her mother before her! Nothing ever stopped Minnow's mother from making the swim each summer, not her tired muscles, not choking on water, not the waves, not the frigid water, nor the great distance. Every year, Marianne reached Picnic Island. And every year, I accompanied her in the rowboat.

"Aunt Anna, could you row beside me while I swim to the island?" Minnow asked me.

I nodded happily. I was honored. It was a favor I would most gladly do.

"Let's go sit on The Rock," Minnow proposed.

For the rest of the morning, Minnow and I sat and talked. The sun, like a giant electric blanket in the sky, warmed our skin. Hundreds of bugs flitted across the surface of the water on their legs of black thread. A school of minnows darted in and out of the underwater crevices of The Rock.

"Imagine living in the birchbark castle," Minnow mused. "You and I could be princesses, Anna. Cliff could be a prince. I suppose Yanny would want to be queen."

There was one problem, I thought to myself. Yanny hated the birchbark castle. She would never agree to be its queen.

"We would reign over the reeds," Minnow continued. "The hummingbirds would be our loyal subjects."

The outhouse could be our throne, I thought, laughing to myself.

"We would need a throne," Minnow said, as if reading my mind. "My rock will be our throne."

Oh, that was a nice morning. Not all mornings were as nice as that one was. I treasure it still.

Around lunchtime, when the loons had moved to another bay to search for food, we returned to the cabin. Minnow skipped up the hill. I walked more slowly, taking breaks to catch my breath. I made my way over to the gladiola garden to pull out weeds. Cliff was lying in the hammock, as usual. He held a fountain pen in his hand and was scribbling on a napkin, making a terrible mess. The nib of his fountain pen dragged on the napkin and the wetness of the ink made holes. Cliff was so engrossed in his writing that he didn't notice Minnow approaching him.

"What are you writing?" Minnow asked.

Cliff looked up, startled. "Oh, my 100-page poem."

"That thing," Minnow said as she perched herself on the tree stump beside the hammock.

"It's not a thing," Cliff answered, cranky. "It's a poem."

Minnow knew not to ask him when he would finish his 100-page poem, so she asked instead: "What page are you on?"

Cliff shifted in his hammock and cleared his throat.

"You can't ask me that question."

"Yes I can. I'm just not supposed to ask when you're going to finish it."

"Oh."

"So what page are you on?"

"Well, the truth is," Cliff said quietly, "I'm still on page one."

"Page one?"

He was only on page one. Minnow couldn't believe it. I couldn't believe it either. He'd been working on his 100-page poem forever. "How long have you been working on it?" Minnow asked.

"Well," said Cliff, with a nervous laugh, "I'm not sure exactly. I think it's been more than a decade. Indeed, it's been twelve years since I started it."

"Twelve years! And you're only on page one!"

"That's true. But it's going to be a good page," he said confidently. "The first page is the most important one. Anyway, Minnow, why do you keep asking when I'm going to finish it and what page I'm on? Ask me something else about it."

"Like what?"

"Like, for example, you could ask what the poem is about."

"What's it about then?"

Cliff cleared his throat again before answering. "I'm not exactly sure yet. But I'll definitely be able to answer that question when it's finished."

Minnow giggled.

"And when will that be?" she said.

"You know I can't answer that."

"Can I at least read what you've written so far?"

"You can read it, yes. In fact, Minnow, you can be the first to read it. But not until it's finished."

Minnow was about to ask when that would be but stopped herself in time.

"Good luck," she told her uncle. "I suppose it's a big project that can't be done quickly."

"Thank you, Minnow."

But Minnow had to have the last word. "Still, Uncle Cliff, I think you should try to get to page two by the end of the summer, okay?"

Cliff agreed to try, but he said there was no guarantee. He resumed writing on his napkin, crossed out what he had written, wrote some more, and crossed that out too. By now, the napkin was a mess of holes and blotches and lines crossing out scribbles.

Minnow dug at the soil with a dead branch. With her free hand, she bit her nails.

"Oh, that reminds me," Cliff said. "I wrote a poem for you earlier." He dug a piece of paper out of his pocket and unfolded it. He recited:

> *I bite my nails*
> *I know I shouldn't*
> *I bite my nails*
> *I wish I wouldn't*
>
> *You see, I'm nervous*
> *All the time*

So I bite my nails
Is that a crime?
I sit on my rock
And I watch a loon
And I bite my nails
From morning to noon

I'm really anxious,
Really anxious indeed,
So I bite my nails
Until they bleed

I bite my nails
I know I shouldn't
I bite my nails
I wish I wouldn't

Minnow held her mouth open, pretending to be insulted. But it was obvious she was delighted by the poem. She gave Cliff a hug, telling him how talented he was, even if he made fun of her for biting her nails.

Cliff smiled with pride. He looked at her messy, curly hair. "Chop, chop," he said, making a scissor motion with his fingers.

"I'll never cut my hair," Minnow said. "And I'll never, ever stop biting my nails."

Cliff looked down at the lake. "I see you enjoy sitting on The Rock," he said.

Minnow nodded.

"As of today," Cliff continued, "The Rock will have a new name. It will be called Minnow's Rock, in honor of you. You sit on it more than anyone I can remember."

"Minnow's Rock," Minnow said, trying out the new name.

"Keep in mind," Cliff advised, "this piece of granite is yours for now, but you don't really own it. Think about the people who rested on it centuries ago! Imagine the people who will gather around it in the future! When everything else changes, this rock remains."

Minnow nodded solemnly and smiled. She was pleased to have the rock named after her, that was obvious. How lucky we were to have her at the cabin. She liked the loons. She liked the pie system. She liked the rock, Minnow's Rock. And she liked the poems. I still have all of Clifferbub's poems. I keep them in a scrapbook so they'll stay preserved.

"Aunt Anna!" Minnow called to me. "Cliff's written another poem. This one's about me biting my nails. And guess what? He's calling the rock Minnow's Rock. Come here!"

I said nothing, of course.

"Are you there?" Minnow asked, scanning the gladiola garden, searching for me.

By the time I emerged from the garden, Minnow wasn't looking in my direction anymore. She was facing the hammock again. I guess she hadn't seen me. I guess she assumed I had gone inside the cabin because she asked Cliff, "what does Aunt Anna's tattoo say?"

I gulped and sped back to my garden, hiding behind the tallest gladiola spike. How did Minnow know about my tattoo? I got that tattoo so long ago it was faded, a light blue smudge on my right arm near my shoulder. I made sure my sleeve always covered it. That girl didn't miss a thing.

"I can't say," Cliff said.

"Why not?"

"Ahhh," said Cliff. "Anna should be the one to talk about it, not me. It's her business. Her privacy should be respected."

"Oh, come on!" Minnow cried.

"I'm serious. If you want to know, you'll have to ask Anna."

Minnow chomped on her nails, then made a declaration.

"I'm going to do two things this summer," Minnow said with determination. "I'm going to swim to Picnic Island. And I'm going to get Anna to talk."

CHAPTER EIGHT
The Arrival of Stanley

Minnow bounded ahead of me, down the path to the lake for her daily swim. At the shore she froze.

A girl was sitting on her rock, picking lichen from the surface, humming.

"Hi," said the girl, loudly. Her hair was blue.

Minnow said nothing.

"You're Minnow, right?"

Not a word burst forth from Minnow's mouth.

"You want to hang out?" the girl asked Minnow, who looked horrified.

At that point, Minnow wished the girl had never turned up, believe me. The girl, after all, had interrupted her daily routine and was sitting on Minnow's prized rock. Minnow didn't answer the girl's question. But that didn't seem to bother the girl, who started talking and who kept on talking and talking.

"I'm bored, and I only got here yesterday. My great-grandpa wanted me to play cards with him this morning, but I refused, so he's playing solitaire. He's boring. I don't know what I'm doing here. I need to be back at home with all my friends. Maybe we could borrow that motorboat from your neighbor and go for a ride. That would be fun. More fun than hanging out with a geriatric."

The girl laughed. It wasn't a nice laugh, more like a snort.

I hid behind a pine tree.

"I'm so hot," said the girl. "Let's go for a swim together, Minnow. But let's stay away from those green things sticking out of the water."

"Reeds," Minnow said.

"Yeah, those yucky things."

The girl jumped into the lake with a big splash and squealed.

By now, I had figured out who the girl was. She must be Nico Marchi's great-granddaughter. Remember? He had said his great-granddaughter was coming to visit, and that she was about Minnow's age.

"It's cold. It's so cold," Nico's great-granddaughter screamed. "C'mon Minnow, get in."

The girl did the dog-paddle, kicking pitifully. Her teeth chattered. Minnow didn't move.

"Minnow! Get in! I'll splash you if you don't. On three! One…Two…"

Minnow ran into the water in a hurry to avoid being splashed. She swam underwater for a long time, like a loon. I suppose she wanted some quiet. It's peaceful under the water, a separate world where no one can splash another person or bother anyone with their complaints. Under the water, no one speaks. People talk too much, more than they need to. That's my opinion, and you can agree with it or not.

When Minnow emerged from under the water, she did a few excellent front crawl strokes, mainly to show off, I think.

"Oh, Minnow!" the girl shouted. "You're a fantastic swimmer. You really are!"

The girl was kind to say that.

"I'm going to swim to that island at the end of the summer," Minnow said haughtily, pointing to the middle of the lake. "It's called Picnic Island."

"No! That far! That's fantastic. You'll for sure make it, Minnow."

The girl had a generous heart, even if her hair was blue.

"We can hang out," said Minnow. "But we can't go out in the motorboat. We're not allowed, and it's not ours anyway. What else do you want to do?"

"Skinny-dip!"

Minnow quickly looked around to see if anyone had heard. "No, I don't think so."

The girl started to take off her bikini top.

"Stop," Minnow said, alarmed. "Someone might see you."

"So? It's not illegal to skinny-dip, or maybe it is, how should I know and who cares?" said the girl, who nevertheless put her bathing suit back on properly.

Minnow peered out at the reeds.

"What's your name?" Minnow asked.

"Stanley," the girl said. "Listen, Minnow. Let's paint our toenails."

"You're joking."

"No, I'm not. I've got a bunch of nail polish bottles at my great-grandpa's."

"Not that. Your name. It's a boy's name."

"So? Minnow's a fish name. Let's write in the sand. Who's your significant other? I'll put it here in a heart with your initials. *Minnow loves—*"

"I don't love anyone," Minnow said. "Not yet."

"Not one? I love six. Sam, Youssef, Blake, Archer, and Ryo."

"That's five."

"Five what?"

"Five names."

"Oh, I forgot Max and Kai."

"Is your grandpa Nico Marchi?" asked Minnow.

"Great-grandpa. Yup."

"He's not boring. He's nice. Now my grandmother, *she's* embarrassing. Sometimes she gets so upset about things."

"Does she use a cane?"

"No, but she keeps an extra pair of underwear in her purse, if you know what I mean."

"Does she play cards a lot?"

"Gin rummy."

"They all play cards. Listen, Minnow. How about visiting the birchbark castle? I haven't been inside there yet. I'm too scared to go alone. Pleeeease."

A smile crept upon Minnow's face. "Yes, we can visit the castle. It's very pretty. You should see the birchbark staircase," Minnow said. "But first let me introduce you to my Great-aunt Anna. She was supposed to meet me here to watch me swim. She's my swimming coach. She should be here soon. Maybe she can come with us to the castle. You've got to keep your top on, though."

"Not another geriatric!" Stanley squeaked. "They all go to bed at eight and wake up before six. They live in a different time zone. Isn't that true?"

"Sort of."

"Anna's the one who won't talk, isn't she?"

"Yes."

"My great-grandpa says she stopped talking the day her husband died."

Oh, dear. The girl had a mouth on her the size of a

garbage pail. I tucked my arms closer to my body to hide myself better behind the pine tree.

"Anna was married?" Minnow gulped. She stood very still.

"Minnow! She's your aunt and you don't know? Her husband died of cancer, exactly six months after she married him. His name was Jacques. Haven't you heard about him? He played junior hockey and he was a goalie and then he became a milkman, because he didn't make it to the National Hockey League. In those days, my great-grandpa says, they used to deliver milk straight to your door."

Here was this Stanley—a stranger—telling my secrets to Minnow without my permission. I felt angry. I should have stopped her nonsensical chatter right away, but I was too shocked to budge.

Stanley was speaking so quickly she was breathless.

"Anna knew that her beloved Jacques was dying of cancer when she married him and she still married him. Isn't that romantic? They lived at the cabin with your uncle Cliff and your grandma Yanny. But Jacques died and Anna stopped talking. She refused to speak a word, starting from the time he breathed his last. She took over his milkman route for awhile after he died. So romantic. She used to go skating in his skates, too, after he passed away. They had the same-sized feet. Then, one spring, fifteen years after Jacques died, she walked onto the frozen lake in the middle of the night in her nightgown and socks under the moonlight and threw those skates into a big crack in the ice. Can you believe these guys used to act like that? She went back home shivering and she woke up your grandma with her bawling and your grandma told her off and said she wasn't the only one who ever lost a husband, because it was the war, you know, and men were dying all over the place, and she was worried about your grandpa who was over there fighting. Your grandma made her swear she'd never venture out on the ice in the spring, ever again, because it's dangerous, and your grandma blabbed the whole story to my great-grandpa later. He told me all this stuff last night. Everyone up here is a blabbermouth, aren't they? My great-grandpa says your Auntie Anna is so nice, she could easily have got married again or done something useful with her life, but she chose to stop living life to the fullest. She became obsessed with her gladiolas to keep her mind distracted. That's romantic, eh?" Stanley let out a deep sigh.

"I didn't know about any of this," Minnow said, her voice trembling. "Not *any* of it."

"I know more than you and I've only been here, like, a day," said Stanley triumphantly. Minnow cast her eyes on the ground.

What Stanley said was true. Except the part about being obsessed with gladiolas. I'm not obsessed. I just happen to have a knack for growing gladiolas. There's nothing romantic about growing gladiolas. It's hard work. I sweat when I do it, so much that my armpits stink. But it was embarrassing, having my past revealed this way. I had to put a stop to it.

I left my hiding place behind the pine tree. Stanley smirked when Minnow introduced her to me. Minnow eyed me strangely, tilting her head as if she was looking at me in a new way.

The three of us got into the canoe and paddled to the birchbark castle. I took the bow and Minnow took the stern and Stanley sat in the middle, blathering on and on about how yucky the reeds were and how yucky the bottom of the lake was and how boring her great-grandpa was. When I turned around to glare at her, I noticed she wore an earring in her bellybutton. Goodness. Not only that, she lilydipped. That was Stanley all right. A skinny-dipper and a lilydipper.

We turned the corner into the next bay. The castle twinkled in the sun.

A few workers were carrying brass beds into a side entrance of the castle. A man with a clipboard was shouting instructions to a group of men and women wearing red T-shirts that said: *Birchbark Castle—Where You Can Be a Royal*. Minnow and Stanley and I hid in the stripped birch woods near the frog pond, watching the action. Our eyes were soon diverted to the lake, where the shrieks of a woman could be heard above the drone of a motor.

The woman was riding a water Ski-Doo or whatever

those little boats are called, careening around and around, leaving sharp waves in her wake. When she hit a wave, she flew through the air and splashed back down on the water with a whack. Every time the machine took to the air, the woman shrieked. I ask you, what's the point of going around and around on one of those cheeky little boats? Where is the talent in it? Me, I learned to row. I learned to canoe. I use my muscles. I still do and that's why I'm strong to this day.

"Wouldn't that be fun?" Stanley whispered loudly, watching the woman in the boat.

Minnow nodded. The woman parked her cheeky little bratty boat at the dock. She strutted down the beach inspecting the sailboats and fishing boats and windsurfers and motorboats. She then marched over the lawn toward the castle.

The woman wore a fluorescent yellow bathing suit with a black-and-green striped life vest over it. Everyone stared at her. Everyone seemed mesmerized by her. She behaved as if she owned the place.

"She's great!" whispered Stanley.

"Yeah, she's great," Minnow repeated in a monotone. Truth be told, I had trouble figuring out what Minnow really thought about the castle. Sometimes she seemed enthusiastic, sometimes critical, as if she wasn't sure what was right, or who to agree with. I guess she was still making up her own mind about it, and that was fine by me.

The fluorescent bathing-suit woman spoke briefly to the man with the clipboard, then she disappeared through the great birchbark front door. A moment later, her head popped out the window of the castle's tallest turret.

"Olly!" she hollered to the clipboard man.

"Yes?"

"I forgot to tell you, when you're in town would you please pick up some marshmallows and hot dogs and drinks for the staff cookout tomorrow? We're having it at noon."

"Okay, no problem," said the man called Olly.

"I wonder who she is," Minnow said.

"Let's ask my great-grandpa," suggested Stanley. "He might know. He spies on the place. He's nosy."

"We were spying too."

"We weren't spying. We were observing."

"What's the difference?"

"Oh, Minnow. There's a big difference."

Nico Marchi was playing solitaire at his kitchen table.

The table was set for two for lunch. His china matched. The china at our cabin didn't match, because we had picked it up at various garage sales over the years. The Marchi place was much more modern than our log cabin. It was more like a house. It had shag carpet, an indoor toilet, a dishwasher and a television.

"Great-grandpa, did you notice that woman out on the lake?" asked Stanley.

Nico smiled a wide smile when he saw me and Minnow. I wondered how I should feel, knowing that he knew all my secrets. I found I didn't mind. It was a relief, in a way. It's painful to keep everything hidden. It's lonely.

"Of course I did," said Nico, getting up to greet us. "It was so noisy I had to shut the window."

Nico set the table for two more people, and my heart leapt through the ceiling with happiness.

"Who is she?" Stanley asked her great-grandfather. "That woman?"

"Her? She owns the castle."

Not only did the woman behave like she owned the place, she *did* own the place.

"I hope I grow up to be just like her," Stanley said boldly.

"Me too," Minnow answered, rather too quickly.

Not me, I thought. Then I realized I was already grown up and I hadn't grown up like her.

Nico stared out his window at the castle. "We have to accept that things have changed on the lake," he said. "We can't spend all our energy fighting everything, the way your grandmother does, Minnow. I'm too old for one of those little boats, but if you two young people wanted to try them, I wouldn't object. It might be fun. Still, they do make a noise. And with that woman screaming away like that, I've got to admit it was hard to concentrate on my solitaire game."

We ate cucumber and tomato sandwiches on whole-wheat bread cut into quarters. Stanley asked Minnow if she wanted to flip through the teen magazines she had brought from the city.

Minnow declined. She said she was going to help her grandmother make an apple pie.

We left Stanley at her great-grandpa's and dragged the canoe back into the water. Nico and Stanley waved to us from the front porch of their cottage. The Marchi place looked like a gingerbread house. The outer walls were painted lime green, and the moldings on the windows were a peach color. The roof rose to a sharp point. The porch was draped in vines. It was a tiny, charming cottage, visited by many a hummingbird.

Little did we know, as we paddled away, that we would never see it again.

great-grandpa are the same age? I mean you and I are the same age, so I don't get it. Shouldn't Yanny be your great-grandma?"

Minnow squinted her eyes and thought, then voiced an explanation. "I think Yanny had my mother late because she waited till after the war. And my mother was really old when I was born, I know that."

"How old was your mother, exactly?"

"I don't know," Minnow said.

"I didn't think old people could have babies," said Stanley.

"She wasn't *that* old!"

"Well, why did she wait so long to have you? There wasn't any war in the way, was there?"

"I don't know why," Minnow said dully.

"You don't know much, do you?" said Stanley.

Minnow said nothing. She blinked, as if trying to stop herself from getting teary.

"Here's one thing I'd like to know more about if I were you," Stanley advised her friend. "It's about your mother and Yanny…"

Minnow leapt off The Rock and waded into the water. Stanley didn't finish her sentence. There was no point, as Minnow was too far away to hear it anyway.

Minnow went for a short swim and returned to The Rock. She didn't look at Stanley.

"Minnow," said Stanley. "Listen to me, please. I'm sorry if I insulted you. Let's walk to the castle. I can't wait to get on one of those fast boats! *Voom, voom.*" Stanley pretended to drive the little boat, squatting down and clutching imaginary handles, swaying from side to side, repeating the words voom, voom.

I sniffed the air. It smelled smoky, like a campfire.

Yanny and Cliff suddenly came crashing down the path.

"Fire," yelled Cliff, his face serious. "Big one. Over in the next bay."

A cloud of smoke hung over the birch trees in the next bay, where the castle and the Marchi place stood. The cloud was a sickly brown color, dense on the bottom and wispy on top. A number of motorboats, likely filled with volunteer firefighters, were speeding toward the bay where the smoke seemed to be coming from. Yanny and Cliff climbed into the canoe and took off without saying a word. They paddled fast. Yanny was wearing high heels and an orange skirt with matching orange blouse and orange blazer. That's a great way to dress for fighting a fire, let me tell you.

I stayed back to look after the girls. Minnow put her arm around Stanley, who was quiet for once.

"Don't worry, Stanley. It's probably just the castle people burning garbage."

"Do you think—do you think—it's my great-grandpa's place?"

"Of course not," Minnow said. "We could drive over there if you want. Will you drive us, Anna?"

I fetched the car key from the hook beside the stove. We all climbed in the station wagon in a hurry, then we sped along our dirt driveway, turning right towards Nico's cottage.

A fire truck hurtled by us on the road. The truck turned at the Marchi sign. Stanley moaned. I felt nauseous. We followed the fire truck down Marchi's Lane.

Nico was helping the firefighters unroll the hoses from the truck.

Smoke rushed out of the peach windows in big puffs. The cottage had already turned black, and was being eaten away, wall by wall, by fire. The pointy roof had disappeared. The vines on the porch were now charcoal.

The firefighters sprayed the fire using water sucked up from the lake. Their faces were wet with sweat. They coughed from the smoke. They cursed at the fire. They worked and worked, for more than an hour. But they had arrived too late. Soon only the frame was left and then that collapsed too. Eventually there was nothing left but burning planks and piles of ashes. The gingerbread cottage was gone.

The firefighters gradually drifted back to the fire truck or to their boats and left. One of them patted Nico on the back. Another told Nico how sorry he was. Another gave a mint candy to Stanley.

One firefighter, Inspector Bonell, remained to try to figure out what had caused the fire. He talked to Nico for awhile. He held up a wet finger to determine which way the wind was blowing. Then he walked over the dried-up frog pond, tramped over the castle's lawn in his big boots, and disappeared through the birchbark door.

Yanny's hair and face and outfit were all smeared in ash. Her nylons were ripped in a dozen places. She wasn't wearing her shoes anymore. Minnow hugged Stanley, who was sobbing.

Poor, poor Nico Marchi. If only our cabin had burnt down, instead of his.

"I took a long walk this morning through the forest across the road," Nico explained. "I was examining the stripped birch trees. When I came back there were flames spewing out of every window. I don't understand it. Thank goodness Stanley was away at your place when it happened. Thank goodness we're all okay. You know, I built this cottage. I can't believe it's…"

He stared off into the distance, trying not to cry.

"You can stay with us," Minnow said quietly.

Yanny, Cliff and I agreed with all our hearts. There was plenty of space. Nico would take Cliff's room since Cliff could spend each night on the hammock. Stanley would sleep on the orange corduroy couch in the living room next to Minnow's brown couch.

Before long, Inspector Bonell returned from the castle. He took Nico aside and spoke to him privately before leaving. Nico walked down to his dock, motioning for us to follow.

We all sat down on the dock in the pink dusk.

Yanny asked what the inspector had said. Nico didn't answer. He closed his eyes and shook his head. Yanny asked him again what the inspector had said. Nico waited a minute before speaking.

"The castle held a bonfire for their staff at lunch," he said slowly. "They cooked hot dogs and marshmallows, the usual. The guests arrive tomorrow, so I guess it was sort of a celebration in advance of the official opening. They didn't put the fire out properly—"

Yanny gasped.

"Let me finish, Yanny. They didn't put the fire out properly, and it spread with the wind to my cottage. That's what Inspector Bonell said. It's been so dry lately the fire spread quickly."

Nico pointed to the right. "Look," he said. "The loons."

We watched the loons floating on the water. We heard them cry, back and forth, back and forth.

"After lunch, the castle people went into town to the bar," Nico continued. "They just got back, actually. So they had no idea their bonfire was destroying my cottage. That's why the castle people didn't help put out the fire, in case you were wondering. Oh, and the castle's intact. The fire didn't touch it."

Yanny threw a fit.

"I've heard enough!" she screamed, pounding the dock with her fists. "I've had it with this castle. First the birch trees, now your cottage. What's next? I've had it. Who would start a bonfire in this dry weather and not bother to put it out and then waltz into town for the afternoon while the rest of the people on the lake are holding the hoses? I've had enough of this castle!"

"Yanny," said Nico. "Take it easy. Everyone's okay, and that's what matters."

"The castle must be shut down!" Yanny said. "Minnow, I forbid you to go anywhere near that place again. That goes for you too, Anna."

It was a sorry afternoon. We returned to the cabin dejected, by car and by boat and by foot. When Yanny arrived at the log cabin she hurried inside and grabbed the purple paddle from the mantelpiece. She stormed down to the beach and marched to the end of our dock.

Clutching the paddle in her right fist, resting the handle on her foot, Yanny stood silently staring out at the lake—at the reeds blowing back and forth in unison, at the rippling surface of the water, at the lone pine tree lording it over Picnic Island. She stood there staring at the lake, with the purple paddle as her staff, long after the sun had gone down.

CHAPTER TEN
Gliding Across the Ice

Stanley lay on the orange corduroy couch, covered in three quilts, weeping and hugging Bow Bow Pom Pom tightly against her shoulder. Minnow had lent her the clown for the night.

Rain pelted the cabin's roof, sounding like popcorn popping. Finally, rain. If only it had rained earlier. The wind whistled through the birch trees. A branch struck the living room window. Lightning flashed, followed by a growl of thunder. We adults played gin rummy at the kitchen table while the girls whispered loudly to each other.

"Aren't you scared?" Stanley asked Minnow after a thunder crack.

"Just think of something unscary, like pies," Minnow suggested.

"Pies?"

"Imagine a lemon meringue pie. The meringue reaches the ceiling. It's a fluffy mountain."

"Sounds good."

"Now imagine a blueberry pie. The blueberries are the size of baseballs, and as blue as, as blue as…"

"As blue as blueberries," Stanley interrupted. "Now imagine an apple pie."

"What about it?" asked Minnow.

"I don't know. It smells good, though."

"It's as big as this cabin," Minnow said. "It sparkles with huge dollops of melted sugar and cinnamon. And it smells like, it smells like…"

"It smells like an apple pie!" exclaimed Stanley.

"Girls!" shouted Yanny. "Enough talking. It's way past your bedtime."

"I can't sleep," said Stanley.

"Try," replied Yanny.

"You wouldn't be able to fall asleep either if your cottage burned down," said Stanley, who then shut her eyes and within a few minutes fell fast asleep. The girl snored like a bear.

The next morning, we ate toast covered in Yanny's homemade raspberry jam. Cliff spilled crumbs all over his pant legs.

Poor Cliff, his face was dotted with no-see-um bites because he had slept in the hammock all night. He said he didn't mind the bites. No-see-ums, he believed, deserve a place in this world. I really couldn't agree. In my opinion, beetles are the most admirable insects. Ladybugs are beetles, after all.

Incredibly, Nico was calm. He said he'd wait a week and then worry about the fact that he no longer had a home. Poor, brave Nico Marchi! As far as I was concerned, he could stay at our place for the rest of his life. Nico was a wonderful man, as handsome as a picture.

The storm of the previous night had ended and the sun was trying to come out. It was a perfect morning to pick raspberries.

Yanny doled out plastic bowls. We walked in a line along our driveway to the part of the road where the raspberry bushes grew. Minnow had to teach Stanley how to pick raspberries, since Stanley, unbelievably, had never done it before. Pull the berries off gently, Minnow explained. Don't take the mushy ones; they're too ripe. Don't take the whitish ones; they're not ripe enough. Check inside the berries. If there's a bug inside, drop the berry, quick as you can.

I think I ate more raspberries than I dropped into the bowl. My hands were dyed red. I could feel the seeds stuck in my teeth, pressing on my gums. The stems of the bushes prickled my arms and legs. The odd car drove by, blowing dust. The sunshine, which had burst through the clouds, warmed my bent back.

Before long Stanley grew bored.

"When I came here, I didn't think I'd be forced to find my own food," she hissed to Minnow. "What will the geriatrics ask us to do next? Make our own fishing rods?"

"Shhh," said Minnow. "They might hear you."

"I don't care. Minnow, are we still going to go for a ride in one of those things?"

"What?" asked Minnow.

"A ride on one of the little boats. Remember? We were going to ask the owner."

"After what the castle people did to your great-grandpa's cottage?" said Minnow, her lips curled in disgust. "We aren't going near there."

"Oh, Minnow. A little boat ride won't hurt anyone."

"Forget it," Minnow said, then walked away from her friend to pick from a different bush.

When we had filled our bowls, we returned home for lunch. We ate melted cheese on bread, and pickles and chocolate pudding.

The afternoon was a lazy one. Yanny went for a canoe ride by herself. Cliff watched Yanny from the shore with the binoculars in case there was a boat ballet incident and she needed to be rescued. Nico lay down on the orange couch and took a nap, which lasted five minutes. He couldn't sleep and I don't blame him. He walked off in the direction of his burnt-down cottage and returned a few hours later with ashes on his shoes. He had sifted through the ashes with his cane, looking for anything that might have survived the fire. He showed me what he had found: two candlesticks, his collection of coins from around the world, and a bellybutton ring belonging to Stanley.

Not a one of his photo albums was found, though, and he was especially sad about that. All his pictures of his children and grandchildren and great-grandchildren were in them. Poor, dear Nico Marchi!

After Minnow heard Nico speak of the lost albums, she ran down to the beach. Thinking she was going for a swim, I followed, but it turned out she only wanted to wait for Yanny to return from her canoe ride.

"Yanny," Minnow said, as the green cedar canoe landed on the beach, scraping on the sand, "do you have any photo albums? I thought maybe you had some pictures of Mr. Marchi and his family that you could give him. He lost all his in the fire."

Yanny sighed. "No, Minnow, but it's nice of you to ask," she said, lifting herself out of the canoe. "I never bought a camera. I never wanted one. I prefer to keep my memories in my head."

"Oh," said Minnow, frowning. "Because I was also sort of hoping you had a picture of my—of my mother, one of her inside the cabin or on Picnic Island or…"

Yanny gazed out at Picnic Island wistfully. "I don't

have a picture like that, no. But I know that Nico did. It was of your mother standing on Picnic Island with the rest of us, right after her swim one year, when she was about your age. I suppose it must have been lost in the fire too."

Minnow scrunched up her face like she was about to cry, but she managed to straighten herself out to ask Yanny what her mother looked like in the picture.

"She was beside the pine tree, I'm pretty sure," Yanny answered. "And she was dripping wet. She looked so cold. She was hugging herself. And it must've been windy, because her hair was blowing all over the place. I haven't seen that picture in years. But I remember it clearly. It was in black and white."

"Was she smiling?" Minnow asked.

"I don't think so," said Yanny. "She looked all proud-like, but not happy. Well, not that your mother often seemed happy. Then again, she must have been exhausted after the swim, don't forget."

Minnow said nothing. She bit her nails.

"Anyway," Yanny concluded, dragging the canoe farther up the shore. "Where's Stanley? Why don't you go play with her? Don't wait for Anna and me. It'll be ages before we get to the top of that hill."

Later, Stanley and Minnow played hide-and-go-seek. Stanley chose to hide in my gladiola garden. Too bad I couldn't talk, or I would have told her off for trampling on my prize-winning flowers.

Hummingbirds darted in and out of the petunias on our front porch. They're hyperactive birds. A bit like Stanley, actually.

Noise could be heard on the lake. It was the sound of little boats whizzing around.

I rocked on a chair on the front porch, looking out at the lake, shivering because the sun was low in the sky. I daydreamed about the old days, the mornings I sat on the snowy shore and tied up my hockey skates with numb fingers. I glided across the lake, stickhandling the puck, sometimes tripping on cracks in the ice and landing on my stomach. Three, four, five, six or seven boys and I usually played a short game before school. We divided into two teams, light-colored scarves versus dark scarves or people who lived in our bay versus people who lived in the next bay over.

Jacques passes the puck to me. My slapshot sends the puck screaming over the goalie's head.

"Nice shot," comments Jacques as he skates past me.

"Thanks," I say, lightly punching his shoulder.

"Maybe you'll make it into the National Hockey League. You could be the first woman."

"Maybe I will," I tell him, smiling.

If only Jacques hadn't died. If only I hadn't stopped talking. If only, if only, if only…

Yanny emerged from the cabin, banging the screen door and waking me from my daydreams.

She was holding the purple paddle. "Want to watch the sunset?"

I nodded my head.

We walked down to the lake and along our dock. It was getting old, our dock. It was sinking into the lake. Yanny held the purple paddle up to the sky.

"Your gladiolas are looking good, Anna," she said.

I smiled, happy that my flowers could distract her from her worries. The gladiola competition was to take place in a week and I was ready for it. There was little doubt in my mind; I knew I would win again.

CHAPTER ELEVEN
The Gladiola Contest

The fair was noisy and dirty, just as fairs should be. Food stands sold the usual junk, like pink popcorn and apples dripping with caramel. Gambling booths offered prizes of giant stuffed animals and a chance to lose all your pocket change. Dazed riders spilled out of the cages that had spun them round and round and upside down. The mayor of the town was shaking on the seat of a dunk tank, her hair sopping. People lined up to throw a base-ball at a target, and if they hit the target the mayor's seat dropped from under her and she fell into a tank of cold water and got a soaking. After the tenth dunk she took a break. She was still smiling. When you're a politician, it helps to have a good smile.

Stanley and Minnow were deep in discussion outside a booth.

"It won't hurt," Stanley said.

"You do it," Minnow said. "I don't feel like it."

"Come on, Minnow, we'll do it together. Besides, I'm not getting one if you don't get one," said Stanley, "and I really want one, so don't let me down."

"No, don't try to make me."

"It'll look great on you. Come on, you're never any fun."

They were talking about getting temporary tattoos. Finally, Minnow gave in. It's hard to argue with Stanley. She's so persistent.

The girls leafed through a book of tattoo designs, which was full of snakes blowing fire, cherubs, throbbing hearts, elaborate butterflies and flowers upon flowers. Both Minnow and Stanley chose tattoos of roses in full bloom. They stuck their tattoos on their ankles.

"They look so fake," Stanley complained. "What a rip-off."

"I feel different. I feel older," Minnow said. "I hope it'll wash off soon."

We were on our way to the horticulture exhibit for the most exciting part of the fair—the gladiola competition.

As you know, growing flowers was something I did well. I wasn't a great talker, but I grew the nicest gladiolas on Birch Lake, and no one would argue with that. Every year, my competitors would ask me questions. Questions like: "What kind of manure do you use?" or "Are the seeds imported?"

I would grin, saying nothing. The fact was, I didn't do anything extra-special with my gladiolas. I watered them when the earth was dry and sheltered them with a tent made of blankets when the radio warned of frost. I planted them in a place where they had a good view of the lake. I monitored their progress three times a day, sometimes more. I sat beside them to keep them company, which helped encourage the ones that weren't growing so well. I thought about how beautiful they were. I took pride in them.

I had no idea why they turned out so well.

I was particularly proud of my gladiola that year. The stem stood tall, unbowed. The flowers surrounded the stem from top to bottom like a glorious halo. The yellow petals curved outward delicately. The result was a gladiola bursting with beauty. It was the best gladiola spike around.

Nico Marchi had also entered the gladiola contest. Poor, dear Nico. His flower was covered in a thin layer of ash. A petal was missing. The stem was short and drooped. After the fire, the flowers in his garden seemed to have lost their glory, as if they were mourning the loss of the potted violets, which had burned to nothing. To make matters worse, he was forced to display his gladiola in a pickle jar, because all his vases had melted and he was too proud to borrow a vase from us.

Nico was so nervous about the gladiola contest he

didn't want to watch the judging, so he hobbled over to the cooking demonstration at the other end of the fair building. Stanley didn't stick around either. "Bor-ing," she said in a sing-song voice. She took off for the rides by herself.

It was then that Minnow got her idea. She whispered something in Yanny's ear. Yanny nodded, then squeezed Minnow's cheeks with both hands.

"Be my look-out," Yanny whispered to Minnow.

Minnow and Yanny were up to something. My stomach tightened with dread.

"Look at Nico Marchi's gladiola," Yanny said to me, pointing at the worst flower there. "It's awful."

Only Yanny, Minnow and I were anywhere close to the gladiolas. Everyone else, including the three judges, was hovering around the roses. When the rose competition was over, the judges and spectators would join us at the gladiola table.

It dawned on me what Yanny and Minnow were planning to do.

Yanny looked at me. "Should I do it?" she asked.

I paused.

"I don't have much time," Yanny said. "Can I do it? Do I have your permission?"

I nodded. Of course she should do it.

Yanny swiped Nico's gray gladiola from its pickle jar and stuffed it into my vase. Then she took my beautiful gladiola and stuck it into the pickle jar. Yanny exchanged the gladiolas so swiftly that no one saw her do it, except Minnow and me. Even with her arthritis, Yanny could move quicker than a hummingbird, especially when she was up to something.

"It's only because we want to do something nice for Mr. Marchi, so don't tell anyone, Anna," Minnow warned me. As if I would tell anyone.

The judges arrived, looking somber, the way judges should look. Yanny stared off in the distance and whistled to look innocent. When they had examined each and every gladiola, they huddled in a circle to consult. The judge carrying a clipboard announced there was a new winner this year. She placed ribbons on three of the vases—first, second and third place. The judges then marched off to the carnation contest. The spectators followed.

That left Yanny, Minnow and me all alone again.

Yanny glanced around to make sure no one was looking and returned the gladiolas to their original spots. That meant my beautiful gladiola was back in my beautiful vase, and Nico's ashen gladiola was back in the pickle jar.

"Perfect," said Minnow.

"Anna didn't mind, did you Anna?" Yanny said. "Anna has enough ribbons anyway. There's no more room on her dresser for all those ribbons, isn't that right Anna? What's that on your ankle, Minnow? You got a tattoo? Who said you could get a tattoo? We have enough tattoos in this family. Anna has a tattoo on her arm, and it'll never come off."

"Mine's temporary," Minnow said.

"Oh, well, then I think it's pretty."

Nico returned from the cooking demonstration, where he had learned how to carve carrots into fancy shapes. He turned his eyes toward the gladiolas. He seemed puzzled. He took his glasses out of his shirt pocket and peered at the flowers more closely. On the pickle jar was a first-place ribbon.

"First place?" he asked, shocked.

"Congratulations!" Yanny exclaimed with a huge smile.

"But I don't deserve it," said Nico, still stunned. "Look at Anna's gladiola. She didn't get a ribbon, and hers is the nicest, by far the nicest. How could this be? There must be a mistake."

"No mistake," Yanny said.

"But—"

"No buts. I heard those judges talking amongst themselves about your gladiola. They said it was melancholic and vulnerable. They remarked upon its sad beauty. They said they didn't want perfection this year. They were looking for something more real."

"Really?"

"Would I lie? The head judge was nearly in tears when she saw your gladiola, so beautiful did it seem to her."

Minnow nudged Yanny, trying to hint to her that she had said enough.

Yanny continued. "I tell you, Nico Marchi, your gladiola touched the judges' souls."

"Isn't that amazing?" sighed Nico. "First place."

"Amazing and wonderful," Yanny said.

"Yikes, cut," Minnow whispered to Yanny.

Me, I was glad Yanny and Minnow had switched the gladiolas. Nico deserved a bit of good fortune after what had happened to his gingerbread cottage. And it was true: what did I need another ribbon for?

"Let's find the woman who guesses your age," suggested Yanny. "I look much younger than I really am, so I'm bound to win."

We found the woman beside the bingo hall. This woman was known to be a great guesser of ages. Even if she was only a year off, you won a prize. Yanny gave her two dollars. The woman pinched Yanny's cheeks. She peered deep into Yanny's eyes. She stood back and looked Yanny up and down.

"You're eighty-six," the woman said with confidence.

"Eighty-six? My goodness, I'm not that old. I thought you were a good age guesser. Didn't you look at my legs, how exquisite they are? Eighty-six! Imagine guessing eighty-six! I'd be insulted if it wasn't so ridiculous!"

Yanny unzipped her purse and removed her birth certificate from her wallet, as proof of her age. She slapped the birth certificate into the woman's hand.

"We've got a winner," the woman yelled, unhooking a stuffed animal from the rack above her head. It was a stuffed dinosaur.

"How old are you, anyway?" Minnow asked her grandmother as we all sauntered toward the rides. The sun was starting to set.

"I'm only eighty-five," Yanny said. "That woman should go back to age-guessing school."

The lights of the Ferris wheel flicked on.

Nico left us to find Stanley.

"Are you sure that tattoo is going to wash off?" Yanny asked.

"Yeah," Minnow replied.

"That castle is breaking my heart," Yanny said.

"There's nothing you can do about it," Minnow said.

"Who do those castle people think they are?"

We reached the Ferris wheel, offered our tickets to the man who ran it, and climbed aboard.

As we soared toward the sky, Minnow asked, "Yanny, did my mother ever sit on The Rock?"

Yanny didn't answer. Perhaps she didn't hear Minnow over the loud music that was playing below. Perhaps she didn't feel like answering.

The Ferris wheel stopped to pick up more passengers, leaving us swinging at the pinnacle. Yanny raised her eyes to the sky and said, "I wish I were a bird."

"Look at the sunset," Minnow said. "There's just a

sliver of red left. It's sinking…It's sinking…It's sinking… It's gone."

"I wish I were a heron," Yanny said. "They look ancient, but they're strong and beautiful."

"I'd rather be a loon," Minnow said.

I'd like to be a hummingbird, I thought. They go places.

The ride ended in the dark. We staggered off, feeling dizzy, and walked silently to the lemonade stand, our designated meeting place. Nico had found Stanley waiting in line for the roller coaster. We piled in the station wagon and went home, where we found Cliff asleep on the hammock amidst a cloud of insects. He had missed the fair, choosing instead to work on his 100-page poem. Yanny took her dinosaur to her room. Nico proudly set his first-place ribbon on the mantelpiece.

"Pickle jars make good vases," he laughed.

CHAPTER TWELVE
Falling Off

Minnow kicked her legs forcefully. Her arms spun like windmills. Her head turned gracefully when she took a breath. She swam for an hour beside the reeds before breakfast, doing lengths as if she were in a pool. The loons watched her. Their black necks gleamed in the early morning sun.

Minnow waded over to The Rock to dry off. Stanley was sitting on it.

"I have a plan," Stanley said.

Minnow clenched her fists at her sides, obviously upset to find Stanley on her rock.

"Today's the day," Stanley said.

"Today's the day for what?"

"For us to try out one of those cute boats."

Minnow kicked a wave with her foot. "Out of the question."

"We'll ride it into town," Stanley continued. "We could go for milkshakes somewhere. It'll be fun."

Minnow sighed.

I heard the whole conversation even though I wasn't eavesdropping or hiding behind a tree. The girls simply forgot I was around. People often forgot about me because I never spoke.

"We can easily convince that woman at the castle to lend us one," Stanley explained. "They have lots of boats over there. More than they need. Just let me do the talking."

"Do you honestly think she'd let us borrow it, just like that? You think she'd lend something that expensive to a couple of kids?"

"Yeah, I do," Stanley said.

Stanley told Minnow she was tired of playing cards and sitting on a dumb rock. Life is short, she said, and the days are long. She accused Minnow of being boring, of not knowing how to live life to the fullest.

"So are you in or out?" Stanley asked. "In or out? Make a choice."

Minnow bit her nails.

"Out."

I don't know when Minnow changed her mind. She said the word 'out' quietly, as if she wasn't sure. Maybe she got tired of Stanley's taunts about her being no fun. Anyway, she and Stanley did borrow one of those water gizmos from the castle woman that afternoon, and they did take it out for a ride. I would have stopped them if I had known.

Minnow told me the broad strokes of the story later, and I let my imagination fill in the details.

She and Stanley walked to the castle together along the forest trails. No one saw them leave. They found the castle's owner sunbathing on the front lawn, wearing her fluorescent yellow bathing suit. Her hair was perfectly combed. Her toes were painted ruby red. Her eyes were closed. By this time, guests had arrived at the castle. The guests were lollygagging on the new chairs or setting up windsurfers or playing volleyball, shrieking with laughter.

"Hi, Miss?" Stanley said.

The owner opened her eyes and sat up on her elbows.

"Hi," the owner said.

"Quite a popular spot," Stanley commented.

"We've got loads of guests this week. Most of them are in meetings now, inside."

"Such an awesome view," Stanley said.

"It is, isn't it? What can I do for you?"

"Well, we were wondering," began Stanley.

Suddenly, Minnow was angry. Why was Stanley being so nice to the woman, going on about the awesome view? The view of the lake *was* lovely, but what about the view of the nearby woods? The birches had been stripped because of the castle. Minnow couldn't stop herself. She had to say it.

"We were wondering why you took the bark off the birch trees," Minnow said quickly.

"Minnow!" cried Stanley.

Minnow couldn't believe she had said what she said. The words just came out on their own. It was as if Yanny's opinions had invaded her body. Now the woman would never lend them a little boat. Stanley won't forgive me, Minnow thought.

The owner stared at Minnow. "We plan to replant some trees," she said coolly. "No need to worry."

Minnow looked at the ground.

"Actually, what we were wondering—" said Stanley.

But Minnow was still angry. Why was she so scared of this woman? Because of her and her castle, the Marchi cottage had burned to a cinder.

"We were wondering why the bonfire wasn't put out properly," Minnow said.

"Minnow!" exclaimed Stanley.

Minnow put her hand over her lips. She couldn't believe herself. She wished she had kept her mouth shut. Yet at the same time, she was glad she had spoken out.

The owner spoke lightly. "I regret that unfortunate event occurred," the owner said.

There was no stopping Minnow now.

"*Unfortunate*? Nico Marchi lost his whole house!" she

shouted. "He lost everything, even his violets. He lost everything except two candlesticks and a coin collection and a bellybutton ring and that's all. He lost his photo albums, all of them! You call that unfortunate? I say…"

Stanley gave Minnow a look. Minnow stopped talking.

"One day, you girls might be able to work here at the castle," said the owner, forcing a smile. "When you are a bit older. Would you like that?"

"Yes, we would. We would really like that, wouldn't we Minnow?" Stanley said. "Thank you."

"I need hard-working people. You both look like good workers to me. And it's been very nice talking to you."

The owner lay down on her towel again and placed a newspaper over her eyes to shade the sun.

Stanley said: "Yes, well, we won't disturb you. You must need your rest, running a huge place like this. But what we were really wondering, what we actually wanted to ask you was…"

The owner removed the newspaper from her eyes, frowning. "What is it?"

"Could we borrow one of those loud little boats?" Stanley said finally. "We'll take good care of it."

The owner scanned the waterfront.

"Take the one Olly is bringing in, the orange one, get him to explain how to start it. He'll find a couple of life jackets your size. I call them my waterhorses. They're an absolute joy to ride. My guests enjoy them very much."

Personally, I was surprised to learn that the owner had lent them one of her so-called waterhorses. I guess she wanted the girls to stop bothering her.

Oh, Minnow knew in her heart it was a bad idea to borrow anything from the castle people. And she was about to tell Stanley she had changed her mind when Stanley grabbed her by the wrist and pulled her down to the lake. Before she knew it, Minnow was running along the castle's long dock behind her friend.

They climbed on the back of the sleek machine with its bright orange seat and bright orange handles. The key was still attached. Olly gave them some instructions. Stanley sat in front. Minnow sat in back. The boat skimmed across the water like one of those insects that scamper on waves.

"Don't let Yanny see us on this thing," warned Minnow.

Stanley avoided our bay so that she and Minnow wouldn't be spotted. She headed into town, hugging the shore, gradually increasing the speed.

The wind tossed their hair. Water splashed their knees. Trees on the shoreline became a blur. The lake seemed smaller. The girls screamed, enthralled. Another, bigger boat passed by in the other direction, full of people having a good time. Minnow waved to them. Look at me, she thought. I'm flying.

"Go faster," Minnow cried, and Stanley complied.

The boat that passed had created a wave.

"Let's get some air," Stanley yelled, driving toward the

wave. "Yeah, air!" shouted Minnow. "What do you mean, air?"

They hit the wave and became airborne. The machine's nose pointed to the sky. Minnow slipped off the back, screaming all the while, and landed in the water. The boat splatted back down on the water. Stanley, who had managed to stay on her seat, circled back to retrieve Minnow.

"Are you okay?" Stanley asked Minnow, helping her back on. Minnow was distressed.

"No more air," Minnow said. "Please, let's go home."

"We'll go home, we'll go slow," Stanley assured her friend. "Don't worry, Minnow."

By the time they returned to the castle, they saw about twenty other machines buzzing around. The guests were going in circles, jumping over waves made by other boats. Minnow covered her ears to block the noise. Stanley steered the little orange boat toward the dock carefully, worried that someone would crash into her.

"At least we did it," Stanley said, after docking the boat.

"Yeah, we did it," Minnow said.

Stanley stayed at the castle to watch a volleyball game while Minnow ambled back to the cabin along the shore.

Yanny and I were chatting on our sunken dock when Minnow finally got back to our beach. Yanny was holding her purple paddle again. She grimaced in pain.

"Are you feeling all right?" Minnow asked Yanny.

"It's my arthritis. In my knees. It can get painful. It feels like my bones are scraping together every time I move."

"Shouldn't you go to a doctor?"

"I have. She says I'm going to need an operation. Knee implant surgery. I'll get new knees, fake knees, made of metal. Then I'll be good as new. Not only that, I'll be part human, part machine," she laughed.

"Will you be able to jump higher?" Minnow asked.

"I don't think so," Yanny said, patting Minnow's head of curls. Minnow ran to get Yanny a chair from our beach. She dragged it to the dock. Those chairs are heavy, and Minnow wasn't very big. It took her awhile. What a nice gesture!

Yanny sat down and hugged the paddle. "Minnow, let me tell you about the purple paddle," she said. "Things you don't know about it."

Minnow perched on the arm of her grandmother's chair.

"There used to be a dead black cherry tree on Maude Laska's land. That's where she got the wood to make the paddle. She cut down a lower branch of that black cherry tree and took it to the lumberyard and the folks at the lumberyard made it into a board for her. That was about three years ago. She made the paddle in her husband Joe's workshop. He's in a seniors' home now. You might have seen him at the funeral.

"Anyway, Maude used a saw and a wood file to make the paddle. Just a saw and a wood file. She wore thick gloves and a mask to block the dust. I visited her once when she was working on it. Her hair was covered in sawdust. I couldn't believe she had undertaken such a proj-

111

ect. When Maude was a kid, she was the type who played with dolls all the time, talking to them and dressing them and bathing them and pretending she was their teacher. Maude cried if she scraped her knee. And there she was, an old lady in her husband's workshop, making a paddle from scratch. A real carpenter. I asked her how she learned to do it. And you know what she said?"

"What?"

"She said she taught herself. She said it was easier than sewing."

Yanny took a big breath, closed her eyes momentarily, then continued her story.

"Maude didn't varnish her paddle, like you're supposed to. She painted it purple instead. I told her to let the wood show. But she said she always wanted a purple paddle. That was Maude Laska for you. She was so fanciful. And the funniest part was that she wasn't a very good paddler. I was much better, you know. She always took the bow and I took the stern. She couldn't do the J-stroke properly, no matter how many times I showed her! Oh, she was a lily-dipper. The lillydipper of lillydippers. I asked her why she wanted to make her own paddle and she said, 'Oh, Yanny, I just wanted to make my own paddle, that's all. There's no reason for it.'"

The lake buzzed with the sound of boats.

"This paddle," Yanny said, raising her voice so she could

be heard, "is the best gift I ever got…No, not the best. The second best. You were the best gift, Minnow. You don't know how long I waited for you to be born. Years and years. I never thought I'd have a grandchild. Your mother wasn't the type to settle down and have a family, that's my guess. Of course, she changed her mind when you came along, don't you worry about that. Yes, when you came along, it was a surprise to everyone. And all was well with the world."

Yanny gave the paddle to Minnow to hold. It was a bit crooked, the purple paddle. The paint was chipping off. A crack was developing on the handle. As Minnow paddled through the air for practice, Yanny asked her, "So did you have a good time riding on the castle woman's boat today?"

Minnow seemed startled. She looked like she was going to be sick. She ran off the dock and up the hill.

How did Yanny know about what Minnow had done? I didn't even know about it at the time. Yanny should have minded her own business more. It wasn't illegal to ride one of those personal watercraft thingies. A lot of people did it.

"What did I say?" asked Yanny. Then she slapped her thigh and said, "I could kick myself for upsetting Minnow."

I followed Minnow to make sure she was okay. She had stopped where Cliff was lying in the hammock.

"Minnow! What's the matter?" he asked.

"Why are you always lying on that hammock?" she shouted. "Why don't you do something with your life?"

"I've done a lot with my life."

"Like what?"

"Like I finished page one today."

Minnow couldn't help it. She had to smile, even through her tears.

CHAPTER THIRTEEN
Bread and Milk and Poetry

The front door banged shut in the night. I woke up with a start, swung myself out of bed, and peeped out the window to see who was there. It wasn't a robber. It was just Minnow and Stanley, tiptoeing to the outhouse in their bare feet under the light of the moon.

I chuckled. You can bet those girls were scared, having to go to the outhouse in the dark. The outhouse wasn't a pleasant place at night. It was full of mice. Cobwebs slung over the seat. The door creaked. And because there was no window, the hut was so dark inside that it was hard to find the toilet paper half the time. It also smelled bad, as you can imagine. The trick was to take a big breath before entering, dash inside, then try to hold your breath for as long as humanly possible.

At least Minnow had a friend at the lake. It's nice to have a friend, especially when you have to go to the out-house in the middle of the night.

The geriatrics were in for a surprise the next morning. Yanny saw it first. She burst out of the outhouse hollering, making little sense.

"A window! Not a sun peeking. Who did it? I did not ask for a—We never—! I wanted clouds!"

After years of debate, our outhouse finally had a win-dow. It was not cut in the shape of a sun peeking out from behind clouds. Nor was it a cabin next to two pine trees. Nor, I must add, was it a bouquet of wildflowers.

It was a square.

A plain old square.

I knew who had done it and when they had done it and I thought it was a clever joke the girls played on us, so I kept their secret. It was a wonder no one heard them out there sawing, but then there was a wicked wind that night, winding through the trees. Anyway, Yanny blamed Cliff. Cliff blamed me. Minnow and Stanley giggled the morning away. They never did own up to their prank. All I can say is that I'm glad we finally got a window, even if it wasn't the shape I wanted.

Yanny couldn't get over it, though. "No one ever sug-gested a square!" she said. "A sun. A bouquet of flowers.

A cabin next to two pine trees! But not a square. Never a square. I would have settled for a bouquet. I would have settled for a cabin. But not a square. A square is simply not creative!"

I went out to tend to my potato plants. Did you think I only grew flowers? I'm a good potato-grower, too, although I never entered a potato of mine into any contest. I'll admit potato plants aren't very pretty, but they do help put food on the table. Cliff returned to the hammock but of course you're not surprised about that. He scribbled away on a napkin, his wrinkled hands shaking with age. Minnow sat on the tree stump beside him. She was wearing one of Yanny's flowery skirts, because all of her own clothes were in the laundry basket. The skirt flowed past her ankles. We needed a trip to the laundromat.

"Working on page two?" Minnow asked Cliff.

"The beginnings of a great page," he answered.

"Do you know what the poem's about yet?"

"I think it's about life," he said. "But I won't know for sure until I'm finished."

"I won't ask when that will be," she laughed.

"You can ask, but I won't answer." He smiled, then cupped a hand around his ear. "Minnow, listen. What do you hear?"

Minnow listened. The lake was quiet. The waterhorses seemed to be resting.

"I don't hear anything," she said.

"Exactly," Cliff said, returning to his poem.

He wrote two words in the top right corner of the napkin—milk and bread.

Minnow snuck a peek at the page. "So the second page is about food?" she asked, fishing for information.

"What? Oh, no, that's just my grocery list. We're out of bread and milk."

Minnow watched a line of ants marching over her foot.

"Why did you ask me that?" said Minnow.

"Ask me what?"

"Ask me what I heard," Minnow said.

"Oh, that," said Cliff, shifting in his hammock. "It's just that I haven't heard the loons in awhile."

A feeling of dread passed over me. Cliff knew the loons better than anyone. He watched for them in the morning and in the afternoon and at dusk, often using binoculars. If the loons were missing, Cliff would be the first one to know about it.

Minnow chomped on the nail of her index finger. She doodled in the sand with a stick. Then she threw down the stick and bit her nails again. Were the same thoughts crossing her mind as mine? Lately, the loons had had to dodge a few boats from the castle. Loons appreciate peace and quiet. Maybe the lake was becoming too noisy and too dangerous for them.

"Don't worry, Minnow," said Cliff, who had also noticed Minnow biting her ragged nails. "I know for a fact the loons have relatives on the next lake. They're probably just visiting them."

Minnow returned to doodling in the sand with the stick.

Cliff groaned, rubbing his back.

"What's the matter?" asked Minnow.

"My back," he said, "it aches."

"You should get more exercise, Uncle Cliff," Minnow advised. "Want to go for a walk on the road?"

Cliff said no. He said he had planned to write a new poem for Minnow and couldn't afford to take a break. There was no time to waste.

"What about page two?" Minnow asked.

"Page two can wait," said Cliff. "I've got the rest of my life to finish only ninety-nine pages."

I stopped listening to his tittle-tattle and turned my attention instead to potato beetle larvae. Potato beetle larvae, if you've never seen them, are slimy, pudgy, soft orange critters that chew big holes in potato leaves. The beetles keep chewing on the leaves until there are no leaves left to chew. To save my potato plants, I had to collect the beetles in a jar, gently so they wouldn't be injured. Then I dumped them under the birch trees behind the cabin. Yanny and Cliff never helped me with this job. They didn't like getting beetle goo on their hands.

"Lots of potato beetles today?" Minnow asked me, having grown bored with Cliff.

I nodded. "You know, Anna," said Minnow, "if you

learned how to talk again, you could have a conversation with Nico Marchi."

I almost smushed a potato beetle with my thumb and usually I was so considerate with them. That's how upset I was about what Minnow had said. Wasn't she full of advice today?

"I could help you," Minnow said. "We could start slowly, with easy words. It will take time for your vocal cords to warm up."

I tried to ignore the girl. I couldn't possibly talk again.

"Wouldn't life be easier if you talked? Well, wouldn't it?"

She was starting to rattle my nerves.

"So you won't learn to talk?"

I shook my head no.

"People around here don't do much to improve themselves," Minnow murmured. "I'm going to sit on Minnow's Rock for awhile, by myself. Don't tell Stanley where I am."

Poor Stanley. Minnow didn't want to share The Rock with anyone.

By the time Minnow returned from her rock, Cliff was snoring. His napkin was blowing in the breeze on the ground underneath the hammock.

"Where am I?" he shouted as Minnow shook his shoulder. When he was fully awake, he laughed, realizing he was simply on the hammock.

"Did you finish the new poem?" Minnow asked.

"Yes," he said, frowning at his empty hands. "But I've lost it."

Minnow crawled under the hammock to get the napkin.

"This poem," said Cliff, "is about a rock. A very special rock." He cleared his throat. He held up the napkin. When he read, he seemed more out of breath than usual. Perhaps he was nervous. Or not feeling well. I'm not sure which.

He read:

> *Immovable is the callused rock*
> *Perpetual place of calm*
> *A girl ascends*
> *Settles there*
> *Safe.*
> *O solid home*
> *On Birch Lake*
> *Our lichen-covered throne.*

Minnow paused for a moment to make sure he was finished, then she clapped madly. The poem surprised me. So many big words—too many, in my opinion. Still, it had a nice feel to it. And Minnow seemed impressed, judging by her strong clapping.

Suddenly Nico Marchi appeared next to me, smiling. I was holding my jar of beetles, not looking too pretty. If only I was wearing a skirt like Yanny. But Nico Marchi didn't seem to care.

"Would you like to go for a walk on the road?" he asked me. He swung his cane, seeming so glad to be alive.

Did I want to go for a walk with Nico Marchi? Did loons like water? Did hummingbirds fly? Was Bow Bow Pom Pom a clown? I nodded, raised my hands to show him the beetle goo, traipsed to the cabin to wash up, then returned to where he was standing waiting for me.

The rain started when we reached the road. But we didn't turn back. We kept on walking, arm in arm. He didn't kiss me that day, in case you were wondering.

The kiss came later.

CHAPTER FOURTEEN
The Log Castle

It was a cry of anguish, rising from the shore.

I scrambled out of bed to see what the matter was. So did Nico and Minnow and Stanley. Cliff rose from the porch rocking chair, where he had slept. We raced down the path to the lake. It had stormed all night. Tree branches that had snapped in the storm lay across our path, blocking our way. Minnow and Stanley jumped over the downed branches. We oldsters crawled over them.

Yanny was sitting cross-legged on the wet sand, crying.

"The purple paddle," Yanny sobbed. "It's gone."

How could it be gone? As far as I knew, Yanny kept it safe on the mantelpiece inside the cabin, except when she carried it down to the dock every night and held it up to the sky.

"I didn't bring it up to the cabin last night," Yanny moaned. "I left it under the canoe because I was going to take a canoe ride this morning. Now it's gone."

The purple paddle was indeed gone. We couldn't see it anywhere. We tried to comfort Yanny. The waves created by the storm last night probably carried the paddle off, Cliff explained. He assured Yanny that we would find it washed up on shore somewhere on the lake. We all agreed to help search for it. We would hunt for it in every cranny of the shore. We were determined to find the paddle. After all, Maude Laska had made it from scratch with a saw and a wood file, and she had painted it purple and given it to Yanny in her will.

Cliff organized the search party. Nico and I scouted the shore to the left and right of our property. The two of us walked cautiously in the shallow water over the rough pink stones, looking for anything purple. We had to hold hands because Nico had problems with his balance, you see.

Stanley volunteered to borrow one of those horrible little boats from the castle's owner to search the area near town. "All this commotion over a lousy paddle," Stanley muttered to Minnow. "Your grandmother should try to take it easy or she'll have a stroke."

Minnow and Yanny climbed into the green cedar canoe to check the area around Picnic Island and the bay where the castle stood. Cliff phoned every resident on the lake to ask them if they had seen the paddle.

The search was thorough, but the paddle was not found. There was no trace of it.

Yanny could not be consoled. She blamed herself for the loss. She said she should not have stored it so carelessly. She said she should have known a storm would carry it off. When she had finished blaming herself, she stopped talking altogether.

"Why don't you make a pie?" Minnow asked her grandmother. "It might take your mind off the paddle."

Yanny glared at Minnow, then stormed up the stairs and locked herself in her room. Cliff banged on the door several times but Yanny wouldn't answer.

Minnow sat down on one of the wobbly chairs at the kitchen table and looked miserable. "This summer has been horrible."

"Oh, Minnow," said Cliff, pulling up a chair beside her. "It's been a wonderful summer. Think about how your swimming has improved. Think about the time we picked raspberries and the time we made a rhubarb pie for Yanny. Oh, there are so many beautiful things to think about."

Cliff turned his head toward the window facing the lake.

"Are you looking for the loons?" Minnow asked.

"You should go play with Stanley, instead of getting all caught up in the concerns of some old people. What does Stanley call us, geriatrics? That's what we are, it's true. Go do something on a lark. Like dig for some clay in the lake and make statues of toads."

"How long, exactly, have the loons been missing?" Minnow asked, as if she hadn't heard a word of what her uncle had just said.

"Four days," said Cliff, still staring out the window.

"Maybe they've flown south already," Minnow suggested hopefully.

"No," Cliff said. "It's much too early. They've gone somewhere else probably. The lake is too noisy now. People can barely talk to each other, never mind write a poem in peace. No wonder I'm still on page two. Now go outside and play. And don't worry."

"Uncle Cliff?"

"Yes?"

"I still think this has been a bad summer for all of you."

"Oh, Minnow, you haven't been listening to me, have you? It's been the best summer ever here."

"The best? How could it be the best?"

"Because you're here. It's the best summer ever, because you came to spend it with us. You're the best."

"Uncle Cliff?"

"Yes?"

"Can I tell you something, if you promise not to tell anyone?"

"Of course, Minnow."

They both forgot I was there, listening to their conversation. That was me—a watcher and a listener, but not a participant.

"Lately," continued Minnow, "I've been having the same daydream, over and over. Do you ever do that, Uncle Cliff?"

"All the time," answered Cliff. "Mostly I daydream about food, like blueberry pancakes and raspberry pies. Sometimes I daydream that I'm a famous poet and that a lot of people drive up here for the sole purpose of hearing me recite my poems. So tell me, Minnow, what is this daydream of yours about?"

"Oh," said Minnow, lowering her head a bit. "It has to do with my swim to Picnic Island. It's so stupid. I daydream…I daydream that when I reach the island, my mother is there waiting for me. Is that stupid?"

"It's a wonderful daydream, Minnow."

"Uncle Cliff?"

"Yes?"

"Do you think Yanny knows about the loons?"

"Maybe. Maybe not. But don't tell her, just in case she doesn't know yet. That would upset her to no end."

"Could you write a poem for her? That always cheers me up when I'm upset."

"Thanks, Minnow. It's nice to know my poetry does some good in this universe. Poetry is my life. But I know what might bring Yanny out of her funk, and it's not poetry."

"What is it?"

"A strawberry milkshake. It's her favorite thing in the world."

"I thought rhubarb pie was her favorite thing in the world."

"They're tied for first, then. Now let's bring Yanny out of her room and take her to the Foxglove Hotel."

Cliff yelled upstairs: "Okay, Yanny, enough is enough. I'm going to gather up everyone in the search party and drive them into town and treat them to some milkshakes. See you later, then, Yanny. You don't like milkshakes anyway, not at all, especially strawberry milkshakes."

The door to Yanny's room creaked open a little. "Just a minute," she said quietly. "I'll be ready soon."

Yanny emerged from her room with her head held high, dressed in her best pink outfit. She wore her pink skirt and pink jacket and her pink parrot earrings and her pinkest pink lipstick, with a bit of it smudged on her teeth. "Did someone mention strawberry milkshakes?" she asked, trying to hide a smile.

We waited fifteen minutes for a table. That's how popular the Foxglove Hotel restaurant was. After we had got our shakes another group of people entered the restaurant and headed to the table next to us. The people were noisy, talking and laughing too loudly.

"Beautiful day," a woman in the noisy group told us as she passed by to get to her table.

"It's not so beautiful, my dear," Yanny replied.

"Not beautiful?" exclaimed the woman, "But the sun is shining!"

I examined the woman more closely. I had only seen her once before, but I recognized her. I was pretty sure Yanny had never laid eyes on her, though.

"It's true the sun is shining," Yanny told the woman, "but to me, the day is not beautiful."

Nico gave me a look and shifted uncomfortably in his chair. Clearly, he recognized the woman too.

"Good milkshakes, eh?" said Minnow to Yanny, trying to distract her grandmother. Obviously, Minnow recognized the woman too. But Yanny would not be distracted. She had had a bad day. She had lost the purple paddle. She was in a feisty mood, and she wanted to share her troubles with a stranger.

"And why is the day not beautiful, if the sun is shining?" the woman asked Yanny.

Yanny sighed. "Where should I begin?"

"Oh, Yanny," broke in Nico, "you don't have to discuss your troubles here."

"Nico," said Yanny. "With all due respect to you, this woman seems interested. I was just about to tell her why the day is not beautiful."

"You were," the woman said.

"Well, I don't want to ruin your meal with all these problems, but I think people should be made aware. Starting with the noise."

"What noise?" asked the woman, perplexed.

"Listen, and you'll hear the noise, even as we speak, even inside this very restaurant. It's the noise that has been heard night and day on this lake for the past month. It's the noise that has driven away the loons of Birch Lake, who used to enjoy a haven here. It's the noise of the boats, the ones built for one or two people, the ones that look like snowmobiles—you must have seen them. I had never seen such boats until this summer. And who is driving those boats? Guests of that absurd castle."

The other woman blushed, saying nothing.

"Are you new to this area, or just passing through?" Yanny asked, then continued without waiting for an answer. "You would not believe what's going on here. Have you heard about the castle? The birchbark castle? Did you know that they killed hundreds of birch trees to make the walls? Who needed it?"

By now, the crowd at the woman's table was listening bug-eyed to Yanny.

"Yanny," Nico interrupted her, "there's something you should know."

"Yes, there's something you should know," said the woman. She cleared her throat.

"There's nothing I don't know. I've lived a long, long time. I'm going to get a petition going. I'm going to get that castle torn down. They've broken every environmental regulation in the book. Wait'll I tell you about the fire that burnt down the gingerbread cottage, leaving this poor gentleman homeless…"

"Yanny," Nico yelled. "You must stop this, right now."

"Not now, Nico. I'm on a roll."

"But she's the owner," he said, sighing.

"Who's the owner? The owner of what?" Yanny asked.

"The owner of the castle. Her. The woman you're talking to."

"Oh, dear," Yanny croaked.

"I am sorry you don't appreciate the castle," the woman said. Her voice was strained. She held her chin high. "Many people have told me they are happy that I chose Birch Lake on which to place my resort. Others have commented on the castle's beauty. Perhaps we could have dinner one night and discuss your concerns. I could give you a tour. You may change your mind if you're given the proper information."

"I don't need the proper information," cried Yanny, spitting out her words now. "You can't bribe me with your big words and a fancy tour and a dinner of fancy fish and cold soup and perfect rolls and whatever else you eat there! You may think you're the queen of the castle, ma'am, but you're not. If anyone's the queen of the castle, it's me. I live in a log cabin, and it's more of a castle than your birchbark piece of nothing. My room is simple. The chairs around the kitchen table are wobbly, and I go to the bathroom in an outhouse—with a nice window, I might add. But because I have the lake and the reeds and the rock and the loons and the green cedar canoe and the purple paddle, I feel like a queen, and I don't need to live in a monstrosity to prove it. I don't need a castle made of birchbark stripped from the poor trees who are shaking in their booties because they have nothing to cover them. I don't need that at all. All I need is my log cabin on top of a hill."

With that, Yanny got up from the table so abruptly her chair fell down behind her. She didn't finish her strawberry milkshake. Come to think of it, she never started drinking it. She stormed out, making a grand exit, buzzing out of there like a hummingbird onto the next flower.

What happened next was simply awful.

One of the owner's friends giggled. It was just a nervous giggle, I guess, a reaction to a tense situation. But it made someone else laugh. Then they were all laughing. One of them laughed so hard he banged the table with his hand. Another shook his finger at the owner, pretending he was angry at her.

They were laughing at Yanny.

Minnow slowly approached their table, her eyes fierce.

"Don't you—don't laugh at my grandmother," she cried. "She knows more than you." Then she ran outside.

Cliff paid the bill quickly. No one had finished their pricey milkshakes.

I sat beside Minnow on the car trip home. Her arm trembled against mine. We were all silent, as silent as a lilydipping paddle, until Minnow spoke up.

"The day after tomorrow," Minnow declared, "I'm swimming to Picnic Island. I'm ready and I'm going to do it."

Stanley hugged her friend. "You'll make it, Minnow. I know you will."

"Anna will accompany me in the rowboat," Minnow said. I beamed.

"And tomorrow, just for one day, I don't want to hear about the castle and all that. Yanny, you've got to promise. Tomorrow's the day I've got to prepare myself for the swim."

"You can't change the world, Yanny," Nico said.

Yanny was sitting in the front seat with her arms crossed. "The world needs to be changed," she said, earnestly. "In any case, I'll most certainly bake a pie to celebrate the occasion of Minnow's swim. Of course I will, but I don't know what kind yet. Someone better leave something underneath my bed, or how will I know what I'm supposed to do?"

Oh dear, the jig was up. Yanny understood the pie system better than we had realized.

That night, after Yanny had fallen asleep, we placed five items under her bed. I left a raspberry. Cliff left a piece of chocolate. Nico left an apple, and Stanley left a lemon. Minnow hunted in the freezer for a stem of rhubarb, Yanny's favorite. "Rhubarb!" Yanny cried, when she discovered the loot under her bed the next morning. "How thoughtful. Someone left me rhubarb."

CHAPTER FIFTEEN
The Phone Call

Around midmorning, we had a visitor. She arrived along the path by the lake. I couldn't tell who it was exactly, because the birch trees were in the way. I could see that it was a woman, though, because she was wearing a yellow sundress. Her walk was slow and hesitant, as if her shoes weren't right for the bumpy path, as if she feared she was lost, as if she didn't really want to come here, to our plain old shore.

I was the first to notice her, as I was down near the water checking on the blueberries. Let me tell you about blueberry season. It's even better than raspberry season, mainly because of Yanny's pancakes. Yanny makes better blueberry pancakes than anyone else I know. She uses so many blueberries that the batter turns gray, and the finished product has such a lumpy consistency it resembles bear poop. Not that her pancakes taste like that. They taste good. They just look bad.

The visitor stopped walking when she saw Minnow sitting on The Rock.

Minnow sat on Minnow's Rock for hours that day. I suppose she was rehearsing her swim to Picnic Island in her mind, picturing herself struggling toward her goal, beginning with the front crawl and switching to the breaststroke when she got tired, imagining herself getting closer and closer to the island with tired muscles but a happy heart. Or maybe she sat on that rock for hours scanning the lake for the missing loons. Or it could be that she simply daydreamed the day away.

The visitor bent down and undid her sandals and waded into the water toward Minnow and The Rock. Minnow didn't turn around when the woman approached, so she probably didn't hear her coming. Perhaps Minnow chose not to turn around because she thought it was Stanley wading out to The Rock to meet her.

But it wasn't Stanley.

It was the castle woman.

I couldn't believe the castle woman had come. I sped down the hill to the shore, close enough to hear what she might say to Minnow. This time, I was eavesdropping, I'll confess.

The castle woman cleared her throat, and Minnow whipped her head around to face her.

"I like your rock," the castle woman said.

Minnow held onto her rock tightly, her fingers tense.

"Listen," said the woman. "I came to apologize for yesterday, about what happened at the restaurant. My staff shouldn't have laughed at your grandmother like that. They get like that sometimes. They laugh at everything."

"Right," Minnow said, unenthusiastically.

The castle woman chewed her bottom lip. "Is this where Nico Marchi lives now?" she asked.

Minnow nodded.

"Up there?" asked the castle woman, looking up the hill.

Minnow nodded again, and then the castle woman waded back to the shore, put on her sandals, and picked her way up the hill to our cabin. I followed.

And do you want to know what that woman asked Nico? She wondered if he and Stanley wished to stay at the castle free of charge for awhile. She assured Nico her insurance would cover the cost of a new cottage for him, if his didn't. She said she was sorry about the fire. She said she should have apologized sooner.

That was nice of her, I suppose. She was obviously trying to make up for everything she had done wrong, which was a lot considering she had lived here for less than one summer. It was a good thing that Yanny and Minnow told her off at the restaurant. Sometimes it pays to speak up about what's bothering you. Look at how the castle woman was trying to improve herself, just because two people alerted her to the error of her ways.

Still, I didn't think too highly of that invitation to the castle. Nico and Stanley belonged with us.

I had grown used to Nico being around all the time. He had even begun helping me collect potato beetles. And, once I caught him whistling an old tune to one of my gladiolas, the orange one that wasn't doing well. Another time, he sat beside me on the porch for more than an hour as a swarm of dragonflies buzzed around us. He just sat there with me, not talking, not expecting me to talk either.

Nico, of course, declined the castle woman's invitation. He thanked her graciously, explaining he was quite comfortable where he was. When Stanley heard Nico refuse the offer, she had a temper tantrum. She grabbed Bow Bow Pom Pom off the couch and tossed the poor clown to the floor. Then, just as quickly, she picked Bow Bow Pom Pom up again and kissed its dirty cheek. Luckily Minnow didn't see what Stanley had done—Minnow was still sitting on The Rock at the time.

After the castle woman left, Stanley begged her great-grandfather to change his mind. She said it was stupid not to take advantage of the invitation, and she went on and on about it. She said she wanted to live in a castle. She said she wanted to sleep in a turret. She said she wanted to have some fun for once. Yanny told her that life isn't supposed to be all fun twenty-four hours a day, and that if she was looking for something to do, Stanley could help her make a pie. Stanley said she'd make pies when she was an old woman, but not now when she was young and had so many better things to do. Then she tore out of the cabin and sat in our station wagon, listening to the radio at full volume. Finally, Nico and Clifferbub took pity on her and drove her into town.

She was an odd girl, Stanley. She argued with her great-grandfather, giving him such a hard time, insulting him by calling him a geriatric. Believe me, he didn't deserve such treatment from a blue-haired brat. Nico deserved some appreciation, for goodness sake. On the other hand, Stanley came back from town with a bag full of boondoggle and beads and spent the rest of the day making a bracelet for Minnow, hurrying to finish it before her friend's big swim. That was generous of her, I'll admit. Stanley wasn't a mean or jealous girl, just a bit rude, and always looking for excitement when she'd be better off staying put. She wasn't the sort of girl who would contemplate life from a rock, like our Minnow. Not that I'm comparing the two of them—everyone is different and praiseworthy in their own way.

Minnow finally got off her rock in the late afternoon, when Yanny was constructing the biggest pie of her life. I had never seen Yanny so content. That's probably because the castle woman had apologized, meaning Yanny was right all along. And Yanny liked nothing better than to be right all along.

Yanny had decided to make a new kind of pie. She vowed it would be higher than any pie she ever made, filled with rhubarb and apples and raspberries, covered in meringue and dribbled with chocolate and lemon sauce.

Cliff rolled out of his hammock and joined us inside to witness the making of this great pie.

"Remember when I first told you about the pie system?" Cliff asked Minnow. "It seems like such a long time ago. I was still on page one then, wasn't I?"

"How's page two going?" Minnow asked.

"Not bad," said Cliff. "Though I'm struggling with the first line a bit. I might cross it out and start again. I don't think it expresses the true meaning of what I'm trying to achieve."

"Do you know what the poem's about yet?" Minnow asked.

"I'm working on that, Minnow. I'm working on that."

"You could write a poem about loons."

"About loons? I'll give that some thought."

"Or it could be about a family living in a log cabin on top of a hill," Minnow suggested.

"A log cabin!" Cliff exclaimed. "Now that's an idea!"

Minnow laughed. "Well, where does the poem take place now?" she asked.

Cliff stroked his chin in thought.

"It takes place," he said slowly, "here and there."

"Here and there?" Minnow asked, tittering.

"Here!" Cliff shouted, pointing to his heart. "And there!" he whispered, pointing out the window at the sky.

With that, poor Cliff patted his shirt pocket and fished out his pen, then took off out of the cabin like a frog being chased by an over-eager child. We watched him through the window; he was running as fast as he could toward his hammock, which wasn't very fast if truth be told. A marvelous idea must have dawned on him, and there was no time to waste.

Nico then asked, innocently, "When does Cliff plan to finish his 100-page poem?"

Oh, my. We had to explain, just so Nico would know what *not* to ask in future.

The pie-making went on into the early evening. Yanny rolled out the pastry while Minnow hulled the strawberries. Yanny washed the raspberries and peeled the apples while Minnow squeezed the lemons. Yanny beat the egg whites into fluff, while Minnow melted the chocolate. Then Yanny started cutting the rhubarb into bite-sized pieces, and Minnow began asking questions.

"Yanny?" Minnow said softly, "Did my mother like to sit on The Rock?"

It was the second time Minnow had asked that question. This time Yanny answered.

"Your mother?" Yanny replied. "No, not really. I can't recall her sitting on The Rock much."

"Did you?"

"Once in awhile, but not like you do. It's your rock, Minnow."

"Why did my mother leave the lake?" Minnow asked.

Yanny didn't answer. She just kept chopping rhubarb.

"My mother didn't like you, did she?" Minnow asked.

"She liked me well enough," Yanny said, not looking up.

"My mother didn't like the cabin, did she?" Minnow asked.

"She swam to Picnic Island every year, didn't she?" Yanny replied.

"My mother never came back here, right?"

"Oh, Minnow," Yanny said.

"Not since she was a teenager, right?"

"Minnow…"

"What did you do wrong?" Minnow asked.

Yanny stopped chopping and stared Minnow straight in the eye. Minnow had never talked so much before. Usually she kept herself shut up. Now she couldn't stop.

"My mother could have driven me up here, couldn't she?" Minnow continued. "I had to take the bus, just so she wouldn't have to be anywhere near here. She doesn't talk about you, you know. It's as if she doesn't have a mother."

Yanny sighed.

"Am I like my mother?" Minnow asked. "Or am I more like you?"

"Sometimes it seems like I spit you out of my mouth," Yanny answered.

"What do you mean? You mean I'm more like you?" asked Minnow with panic in her voice.

"Is that bad?"

"Did my mother go canoeing with you?" Minnow asked.

"Not much, no," Yanny replied.

"Did she like to watch the loons diving?"

"She wasn't that interested in the loons. If they went missing, I don't think she would have cared."

That was true. Marianne didn't care for the loons. She didn't really care for things like trees or birds or flowers. I wonder if she would have liked the birchbark castle. Probably she would have. She would have admired the birchbark staircase.

"Did my mother like your pies?" asked Minnow, hopefully.

Yanny smiled. "Yes, I do believe she liked my pies, Minnow, although she never admitted it. Her favorite, I'm pretty sure, was lemon meringue, same as you."

Minnow sighed, hearing she and her mother liked the same type of pie. "Do you know what I wish, Yanny? I wish my mother would come back here sometime. Maybe you two would get along. I'd feel better if that happened, you know."

"I know," said Yanny, patting Minnow's hand.

Minnow's eyes were gathering tears. "Because then you and me and her could go canoeing together."

"I know," Yanny said again. "Three generations in one canoe."

"I would sit in the middle," Minnow said. "My mother would take the bow, and you would take the stern."

"Of course I would take the stern," Yanny said. "Who else would stern?"

Minnow paused before her next question.

"Why did my mother send me here for the summer, when she hates it here herself?" Minnow asked.

"When you first got here," Yanny said, "you were thinking she wanted you out of her hair, am I right? That's one reason you were so miserable. But now you know differently."

"What do you mean?" Minnow asked.

"She wanted you to get to know me and Cliff and Anna. She wanted you to know a bit more about yourself, who you are, where you come from. She knows you better than you know yourself, in a way."

"Where I come from? But I come from the city."

"No, you come from here."

"I was born in the city."

"That's just accidental," Yanny said. "Minnow, I have to say that I give your mother credit for sending you here this summer. She must have matured in the past thirty years, to do something like that."

"I used to think you and Cliff and Anna were weird," Minnow volunteered.

"And now," said Yanny, "you know that for sure!"

Minnow laughed.

"And when you're back in the city," Yanny said, "you'll know that there's a rock on a lake that belongs to you, a rock called Minnow's Rock. A person can never lose a rock that big!"

"My mother is nice, Yanny. You would like her now, and she would like you. She's different than you, but she's still nice."

Yanny grunted in agreement. She resumed her rhu-barb-chopping, and Minnow sneaked a lick of the melted chocolate. Then Minnow said she wanted to go down to the shore to search for the purple paddle before sunset. She asked if Yanny could finish the pie on her own with-out her help, and Yanny said yes.

Yanny asked Nico and I if we would give her some time alone in the cabin. I thought that was strange, but of course we did as Yanny requested and got up off the orange corduroy couch.

As Nico and I exited through the front door of

the cabin, I turned around, curious to see what Yanny would do.

What I saw was this: Yanny walking slowly over to the telephone, picking up the receiver, and beginning to dial. She was up to something.

Nico took my arm then, and I closed the door behind us.

CHAPTER SIXTEEN
The Swim

The lake heaved with waves.

Minnow sat on Minnow's Rock, staring at the island, which was hazy in the distance. She jumped off the rock into the water, counted backward from three, and dove in. The waves were frothy with whitecaps. The reeds were being flung about in the wind. The sun hid behind the clouds.

Earlier, Cliff had tried to convince Minnow to postpone the swim until a calmer day. She refused.

"I'm swimming today," Minnow said firmly.

I rowed beside her, watching her struggle against the wind and the waves.

I remembered Minnow's mother making the same swim, year after year, so many years ago. Where was Minnow's mother now? To her, Picnic Island was only a childhood memory. She had moved on and left her past behind. But her daughter was here now, carrying on the tradition. Perhaps one day Minnow's daughter would also make the swim. And Minnow's daughter's daughter.

An object bobbed in the water ahead of us. It looked like a loon. The loons had returned, I thought, elated. They had come back to watch Minnow swim. They wouldn't have missed it. They wouldn't have missed it for the world. But when I rowed closer, I realized the object was not a loon at all. It was a log floating in the waves. My heart sank. Where had the loons gone?

Minnow stuck close to the rowboat to avoid boats, which were darting back and forth, carrying the fool guests of the castle.

She did ten strokes of front crawl, ten breaststrokes, ten strokes of front crawl, ten breaststrokes. Her hair was draped across her face. At first her strokes were strong, but before long she was veering off to one side or the other, finding it hard to keep her course straight. She breathed in water by mistake, coughed, and treaded water for half a minute until she felt all right to continue. She knew that anytime she wanted, she could climb in the rowboat and try the swim another day, and everyone would be just as proud.

When we reached the halfway mark, she gave me a thumbs-up. "Fish are nibbling at my toes," she said, breathless but smiling. "They tickle."

If only I could have given her a word of encouragement. All I could do was nod and grin and give her a thumbs-up. I wish I had Minnow's courage. Imagine making the swim on such a rough day. The girl didn't give up.

After Jacques died, I suppose I gave up. I lost my voice and my heart. I had paid such close attention to my flowers, and—forgive me for sounding corny—I had never allowed myself to bloom.

Minnow was moving more slowly now. We'd been out on the lake a long time, and I let my mind wander.

It was winter again, and I was tying up my hockey skates at the edge of the frozen lake. I left my hockey stick on The Rock and coasted across the ice by myself, under the moonlight. No one else was there, not any of the kids who played hockey, not even Jacques. I skated and skated, to Picnic Island and back. I felt the cold wind on my cheeks. The ends of my hair turned to ice. I skated and skated until my skates were dull. I skated around the entire lake, again and again and again...

Minnow could barely lift her arms out of the water now. Her limbs seemed numb with fatigue.

I could see the shapes of people on the island, waving.

I rowed with my head bowed and caught a glimpse of my tattoo. It was so faded I could barely see the letters anymore. Not even the capital J.

"Keep going, Minnow, that's a girl," Yanny yelled from the island.

Stanley was hopping up and down, chanting Minnow's name.

Minnow was only about five minutes away from her goal.

I gave her another thumbs-up.

Minnow rested again, floating on her back while the waves jostled her. She was so tired that when she began to swim again she did the dog-paddle. She was breathing hard as the waves pushed her back, away from the island.

"I can't," she cried, treading water again, doubt in her eyes.

She dog-paddled toward the boat, as if she was going to climb aboard. But I knew she could make the swim. She was so close. She still had energy, I was sure of it. She just needed a bit of encouragement.

What Minnow saw next must have shocked her. What she heard must have astonished her.

My lips were moving. A choking sound came out of my mouth.

I was trying to speak.

Minnow treaded water, waiting.

What would I say?

I cleared my throat.

Minnow waited.

This is the moment that I start talking again, I thought. This is the moment. I had to say something, anything.

The tiniest of smiles formed on Minnow's lips. She kept treading water, waiting.

But no words came.

My face relaxed. I looked at the sky and shook my head. I would not speak, not now, and probably not ever. I wasn't a great talker. It was too late to change. I needed to recognize that there were things I could do and things I couldn't do. I couldn't talk, but I could shoot a puck and I could grow flowers and I could row a boat beside a couple of girls who wanted to swim far.

Minnow started dog-paddling again, fighting the waves. The shouts of the crowd on the island grew louder, drowning out the sound of the motorboats. She switched to side stroke and muscled her way through the water, getting closer and closer.

"I think I might make it, Anna," she huffed.

When her toes touched bottom, she exhaled, relieved.

"Anna," she said, beaming. "Thank you." Then she took a few tired steps toward the island's shore. Her knees caved in. As she crawled to land, Yanny held out a towel to her. Stanley hugged her, presenting her with a beautiful homemade blue bracelet.

There was another gift too, a wonderful gift.

A woman was standing on the island, obscured by a bush. All that could be seen of the woman, from where Minnow and I were standing, was a mat of curly hair poking out the top of the bush and a couple of white running shoes poking out the bottom, one of the laces undone. Minnow glanced over there, puzzled. Her mouth dropped open. She ran toward the woman and gave her a huge hug.

The surprise was Marianne, Minnow's mother.

Marianne was standing on Picnic Island. She had come home. All was as it should be.

Yes, it was Marianne whom Yanny had phoned the day before. Yanny was right to do that.

The two had had a decent phone conversation, Yanny explained to me later. Not a great conversation, not a good one, but a decent one. Yanny had started the conversation by telling Marianne about Minnow's planned swim to the island.

"Did you tell her I used to do that?" Marianne had asked.

"Of course I told her," Yanny said. "How do you think she got the idea?"

There was a pause.

"Listen," Yanny had continued. "I think you should come here for it, Marianne."

"Go there?"

"To see her do the swim. It's tomorrow. Tomorrow afternoon."

"I don't know," Marianne had said. "I'll have to think about it. It's a long drive." She paused again. "Tomorrow?"

"Tomorrow afternoon. It's not that long a drive, Marianne. You know, if you got up early enough, then…"

"I said I'd think about it, okay?"

"It's important to her, Marianne."

That was the conversation in a nutshell. Like I said, decent, but not great.

It was Cliff who got the call late the next morning from Marianne, who had checked into the Foxglove Hotel in town. Cliff insisted on picking her up there in a borrowed motorboat and bringing her directly to Picnic Island, so it would be a surprise for Minnow, so Minnow's daydream would come true.

It didn't matter that Marianne was staying at the Foxglove instead of our cabin. She came home, didn't she? She was standing on Picnic Island, wasn't she?

"I knew she'd be back," Yanny whispered to me.

Yanny liked to be proven right, and she was right again. Marianne had indeed returned. However, I think Yanny was expecting her daughter to come back a little sooner than she did. After all, it had been a few decades since the girl had taken off in the bus. But never mind that.

She was here, that was all that mattered.

I noticed Cliff looking at the sky. Yanny was also looking at the sky. Soon, everyone was looking at the sky.

A bird flew overhead.

It wasn't a loon.

It was a bigger bird, floating majestically over the island. The bird had a long, long beak, a white neck, and bumpy knees. It looked old. Its wings were the color of dead, gray wood.

It was a heron.

"We've never had a heron on Birch Lake," Yanny pronounced.

"What's that thing in its mouth?" Stanley asked.

"Shhhh," said Yanny, "you'll scare it."

"What has it got in its beak?" Cliff asked, noticing what Stanley had noticed.

"It's a broken branch, I think," Minnow said.

"It's purple," said Nico.

"It's the purple paddle!" Yanny proclaimed.

The heron was carrying a piece of the purple paddle in its beak.

Yanny held her hands over her heart. She smiled. She held up her arms to the sky, palms upward, and swayed like a birch tree in the wind.

"The heron," Yanny said with conviction, "is the spirit of Maude."

I watched Marianne watching Yanny. Marianne was shifting her feet, crossing her arms, looking away, still embarrassed about her mother after all these years. Then, Marianne looked at Minnow, who was watching Yanny. Marianne saw that Minnow didn't seem embarrassed about her grandmother at all. In fact, Minnow was looking at Yanny with satisfaction, as if Minnow agreed that the heron was the spirit of Maude Laska.

Marianne gazed at the waves of Birch Lake, and she squinted her eyes toward the cabin in the distance, and she looked over that way for several moments. Then she marched up to Yanny and I thought she was going to grab her and tell her to stop that ridiculous swaying, but instead, to my surprise, she gently wrapped her arms around Yanny's shoulders and placed her chin on top of Yanny's head.

I won't forget the sight of it, for as long as I live.

After that, Nico came up beside me and kissed me on the lips.

I could hear Stanley making fake barfing sounds.

Remember when I told you Nico kissed me, but I wasn't going to tell you about it? Well, I guess I told you. After all, it was an important event.

The heron flew toward our shore. It landed on a log that was poking out of the water next to Minnow's Rock. The heron perched itself there, unmoving, the purple paddle still in its beak.

This bird had already become the heron of Birch Lake in everyone's mind. It was a proud and fearless bird.

Minnow shivered in her ankle-length towel. "Let's get back," she said. "But this time, I'm going in the rowboat."

Everyone laughed.

"I've got pie, lots of pie," Yanny said. "It's a special pie, in honor of Minnow, who like her mother before her braved the waves of Birch Lake to swim all the way to Picnic Island."

Yanny hugged Minnow and so did her mother again, and then so did everyone else. After that, Minnow shivered no more.

The pie was good, the best pie Yanny ever made.

All this happened awhile ago, five years, really, and I don't remember everything about it. If I forgot a few things, you won't know about it because you weren't there, as I said at the start. I'm sure I missed a few good anecdotes, but you get the gist of it.

Minnow and her mother visit the cabin for two weeks every summer, and when Minnow makes her swim to Picnic Island, I accompany her in the rowboat, which is not just a job but an honor. Yanny and Marianne and Minnow often canoe together too. Minnow sits in the middle, and Marianne takes the bow, and Yanny, of course, takes the stern. It's three generations, in one green cedar canoe.

Yanny still bakes pies and she's still wearing her fancy skirts and she's still running around causing trouble, because she got herself a couple of those brand-new knees everyone's getting.

Nico never did leave our cabin after his cottage burned down. He asked me to marry him and I agreed. I feel so lucky to be with such a man. All the other single women on Birch Lake were jealous and I'm sure they're wondering why he would marry a dame who doesn't talk, but talk is cheap sometimes, I guess.

There's some sad news, though.

Cliff passed away a year ago, died in his sleep in the

hammock with a smile on his face and a hummingbird on his shoulder. Hummingbirds don't stop for anyone, but they stopped for him. He never did finish his 100-page poem. He only made it to page four. I've read the four pages umpteen times but I still can't tell you what it's about. I placed all his poems in a scrapbook and framed the four special pages in a special frame that I spray-painted gold.

It was a sad and lovely summer, The Summer of the Purple Paddle. But it was more lovely than sad.

Every day I pray for the safety of the loons, and I thank the heavens for the heron, who is still the heron of Birch Lake. I give thanks for the pies and the reeds and the outhouse, even the outhouse.

I give thanks also to the castle.

Not the birchbark castle, mind you, but the castle made of logs on top of a hill.

ELAINE MEDLINE

grew up in Toronto, Canada and now lives in the province of Québec with her husband and their dog named Zara. She has three wonderful adult children and three fantastic grandchildren. Her favorite hobbies are downhill skiing, swimming in lakes and going on canoe trips, although her paddle isn't purple. (It's just plain wood). Elaine retired from her career in health care and now has time to focus on her passion—writing. Currently, she is co-creating a short screenplay and finishing her next children's novel.